I0684832

trout
are
Selfish

short fictions and transitions

JG VanDenKooy

This book is a work of fiction. Names, characters, businesses, organizations, places, events, and incidents either are the product of the author's imagination or are used fictitiously. Any resemblance to actual persons, living or dead, events or locales is entirely coincidental.

Copyright © 2018 by JG. VanDenKooy

All rights reserved. No part of this book may be reproduced or transmitted in any form or by any means, electronic or mechanical, including photocopying, recording, or by any information storage and retrieval system, without written permission from the author. For information address the author—jkoiart.com

First Edition
1 3 5 7 9 10 8 6 4 2

Printed in the United States of America
This book is set in 12 point Garamond

ISBN: 978-0-692899-11-3

jkoi // Press

Visit jkoi.art

Contents

Adaption of the MFA thesis
composed at the
California Institute of the Arts
2015-2017
by
Jesse Garrett VanDenKooy

Mentors
Brian Evenson
Janet Sarbanes

Director
Maggie Nelson

Dean
Amanda Beech

"A trout is a moment of beauty known only to those who seek it."

Arnold Gingrich

"To him, all good things—trout as well as eternal salvation—come by grace, and grace comes by art, and art does not come easy."

Norman Maclean

"They've been circling
Since the day they were born
It's disturbing
How they're circling
Fifty feet from the pond...

And they're jumping
And they're jumping
But they'll never get out
Just keep touring
Just keep on ignoring
Be a good little trout

And the butcher stops and winds his watch
and lays their lives down on the block
He raises up his hatchet and
the big hand strikes a compromise..."

Amanda Palmer, *Trout Heart Replica*

Indignation
(stop me if you've heard this one)

It's raining.

A cliché way to start.

Oh yes—and then the apologetic second sentence, that's pretty common too. But now here's something different—a fourth sentence placing a third layer of observation onto itself. How can we analyze what is being said now? Self-analyzing narrative? Self-deprecating narrative? Is it narrative at all, or just some pedantic means of moving forward? Ah, and the deprecation begins, after, of course, introducing the idea.

Yes! So it's self-replicating. That's the answer, and evolving. By now, probably, we've forgotten about the rain. See? Probably: might be deprecating, but it seems like the pedantry is becoming uncertainty. So now it's lost. Oh, that's deprecating. Deprecating deprecation.

Enough. Now it's commanding, self-controlling. But is it self? Whose self? And what is it anyway? Because, I mean to say, it's just text, but I'm writing it now, or reading it, depending on where we are. Or you're reading it, or listening to it. And we have entered the communicative realm. We, you and I. Presently, now. But now when the words were crafted, and now when the words are combined again in the minds of the listeners and readers and re-readers is a different now. But observe, if you will, that these feelings of nowness, and self-evolution, self-analyzation, self-replication, self-deprecation happened at a time that is not your now. For the now to which I refer is here as I write, but I am alone, and I have known this presence, and can exist without the disclaimer, for I am the creator, and so I can say with absolute truth (for I know that I am the exception) that this here, this, and these words existed at a time that is not now. It seems I, and you all, perhaps have once again forgotten about the rain.

It is raining, and to say as much seems far less cliché now, doesn't it? I conclude with gratitude, which is customary, but sincere, as we have shared this now, you and I, and I am filled with joy.

The Generosity of Earl Glover

It was a common era year when Earl Glover, the CEO and President of the chain of companies known colloquially as the Glover Group made his great announcement.

Glover was a complicated man, simultaneously inscrutable and overtly transparent.

In his youth, he had worked hard, doing unfulfilling jobs for minimal pay: a cashier during his time in the city, or, when he could no longer survive in an urban workforce with such high living costs, he cleaned barns on ranches across the Midwest, never staying put for more than a couple of weeks. He did the work, and did it no better than anybody else. The difference was that he did it with a smile on his face. Always a smile.

His attitude was catching. His employers would say that the workforce itself was an engine of esteem whenever he was working. Some disliked the favoritism that Glover garnered from simply because of his personality, but Glover made friends even with those who disliked him, and so his enemies became his friends, a gift that replicated itself many times over the course of his long careen.

He quickly rose to supervisory positions, then oversight, and was picked up and moved from company to company, cleaning up messes and cunsulting with no more intrigue than when he had gone from barn to barn.

He oversaw laborers, and headed a small investment group that funded engineering research. That led him to work as a diagnostic technician at one of the top computer companies, one which he had been fired from in the city years earlier. He held no grudges, though conflict wasn't completely unavoidable.

Glover divorced his first wife after an office affair he had with a partner at a communications firm but remarried some years later when he became the youngest member of the board of directors of a Swedish group of entrepreneurs just breaking in to the worldwide market. After three and a half years he was elected chairman and six years later he sold the company to another group which he would become chairman and CEO of. This group came to be known as The Glover Group when it was named among the top 10 most valuable companies in the country. After having worked as a rancher, IT technician, and director, he now headed up a Fortune 500 company which employed more than 1,500,000 American citizens in factories and workshops across the nation.

After ten years overseeing his business, he made his announcement at one of the largest press conferences ever recorded in American history that was not given by a sitting President.

He was expected to speak, as usual, about the company's progress, quarterly earnings, where it stood among its competitors, but that is not what had drawn the crowd.

Some speculated that Glover would be doing massive layoffs, or that he would announce the opposite and expand into new worldwide markets. The excitement and anxiety around the event generated yet more excitement and anxiety. Glover himself made absolutely sure that every major and minor news broadcasting station was covering his announcement and had personally called many journalists and editors, telling them that this would be the story of a lifetime, and that they would want to be present at the Glover Group's massive pavilion in Northern California. Thousands of media representatives, reporters, network executives, and indeed several members of congress descended upon Glover's Square to watch as the executive stepped up to the podium, put his hands in the air in a welcoming manner that would eventually be the symbol on posters, papers, and propaganda for years following, and speak:

Thank you all for coming today. It is a very special day indeed for all of the businesses tiered within this group. It has been many years since I have shoveled dirt in a ranch, but I remember those days better than some of my days as a corporate executive. I know the value of hard work, and I know even more how little one's hard work is appreciated. This group, he paused, *is composed of some of my very closest friends, all of whom I have made over the years and who have shared my vision. Today that vision is realized.*

Today over 1.5 million people will not be working anymore.

There was silence then, across the nation, stunned emptiness. And then there was uproar.

But Glover continued to speak. Had there been anyone not watching the press conference before, they had started then, prompted by friends, coworkers or news alerts. Radio stations stopped playing music and started a live feed from the speech, and smartphones lit up nation-wide alerting the American people that they faced the largest unemployment rate since the Great Recession as one of the nation's largest conglomerates was about to collapse, dozens of corporations with it.

We have developed the fantastic technology in the past several years, things that have taken a lifetime to build, but are built upon decades of planning for the infrastructure of the future. All the factory workers who are employed by our satellite businesses across the country will be replaced by high efficiency machinery, with the exception of a small team of engineers who will perform regular maintenance. In addition, many services have been perfected and replicated through machine learning. Roughly 99.9% of our employees will stop working after spending the next month or so rolling out this new equipment. The amount of money the company will be saving in payroll alone is staggering, and these new machines will increase efficiency and reduce waste in ways never before imagined on this scale. That being said:

All employees will continue to be paid for the rest of their lives, though they will not ever come to work again.

Was it a joke? The nation was astounded, dumb-founded, confounded; they began to speculate. Some searched for legal ramifications, but every idea that ever came up, every potential flaw in the system, had been carefully considered and was planned by Glover. It was the truth, he had used his power and influence across a vast number of industries and circumvented the government to enact a universal basic income.

He explained that the amount saved on payroll would not go to the company's bottom line. The machines only replaced the workers, but would not need to get paid, so the revenue would continue to be distributed on a regular basis, as before, to the laborers. The increased efficiency and reduced waste would be more than enough to mitigate the investments made to have the machinery built, software programmed, and systems maintained.

It was a huge risk. The entire Glover Group was collateral into this move, and if it failed, it and the 1.5 million employees would fall into ruin.

But this was not the case.

Besides the administration in the corporate sectors of the company and the engineering support teams, the entire company would be machine run, and all labor employees would not have to work for their paychecks. What's more, the additional profit from the increased productivity was allocated by Glover to actually hire additional employees, specifically, low-income or homeless individuals and families. They would be employed and paid by the company without ever lifting a finger.

It became clear what Glover's vision was:

I seek to create a world where we, the people, enjoy the technological advancements not as a means of replacing us, but as a place where we enjoy the fruits of such advancements. If a machine can do a job better than a man, then let that machine do it but only if that man is granted rest from his labors and reaps the rewards.

In an interview conducted only six hours after the announcement, Glover was asked if what he was describing was a kind of pseudo-socialist economy in which large corporations would give an allowance to the people, ultimately compressing the economic structure to a regime not unlike a communist republic. Was this his way of controlling the American people? Would citizens not be allowed to leave the country should they find this new way of life distasteful?

Glover explained that, yes, if one compared this new paradigm to the fallen regimes of the past then people would resist the change. But the truth of the matter was that if you told a parent that they could keep their home and feed their children without having to work eighty hours a week just to get by, then most would grin and tell you that you were, respectfully, full of shit.

But that is the reality of it, and the beauty, Glover said in his interview. *People can rest, and do the things that they could not do before. There won't be an issue of citizenship because this model will produce a global environment that will draw all people to prosperity. The musician who wanted to round up his buddies and start a band can do it and afford it. The fellow who spends his days shoveling dirt but always knew he had a novel in him now has the time to sit at his desk and write. The mother who may have once thought about giving up her kids because she couldn't afford to keep them even with two jobs and pay for day care won't have to make that decision anymore. The only decision to be made now is 'Do you want to have a family?' and now everyone with that desire can say 'yes!' Dreams can be realized by everyone irrespective of the context of their lives.*

Glover was asked if he planned to employ the entire American population.

Of course not. That would be impossible. Sure, we will try to ensure that as many people as possible are getting an allowance substantial enough to survive comfortably. But this will be the new standard, see? Soon every other company will have no choice but to adopt this policy. The people will demand it. Me and my people are simply starting the fire.

And what a fire it started. Glover released his book the following day, explaining how things needed to be handled by other companies and employers as well as by the federal government. It was all spelled-out in terms understandable to the general public and contained the legal documentation to back it up, all while also providing guidelines for legislation bound in 652 pages. Eventually, every citizen would be employed by one of these sponsor companies or 'host companies' as they would be called. Those who performed additional services that could not be done by machines made profit from those positions in addition to their host salary. Those who chose to further their education, and many more would, to become executives or administrators in the host companies could do so and could find luxury beyond the basic host salary if they chose to work for it.

There is no more waste, because everybody has what they need, and more if they want to work for it. Everything is accounted for.

On the third day following the announcement, Glover made his final speech. He announced that he was stepping down from his position and would be running for public office.

On that afternoon he was assassinated.

A single man from the budding resistance that would come to be known as the 'Liberty Caucus' shot Glover point-blank when the man went to shake his hand.

It didn't take long for this renegade group to grow and protest the new changes, but the federal government took them down in what was considered to be the most direct attack on a terrorist organization on domestic soil.

The country started changing after Glover's death, and just as he said it would. He became known as the man who started the second era of American history, the Third Industrial Revolution, and was considered the greatest asset to the country since Henry Ford. America became more than a superpower in the years following the paradigm shift, it became a world leader in exemplary quality of life. When so many people wanted to immigrate to the US from their homelands world leaders had no choice but to cooperate with the American model and adopt the new social regime. It took less than a generation for America to change, and less than two for the majority of the world to adopt it. The world had united under a single creed and truth:

…that no human being be without food, water, and shelter. And that hard work leads to luxury, not to minimum need. All people would give what they have to offer, not for any state, and not for any company, but for one another. The bakers would bake to share their bread only because it brings them joy, and joy to others. People have the freedom to dream, and the security to fulfill those dreams.

The system Glover had implemented and the plan he devised was nearly perfect. Though it, like all systems, was subject to the entropy that invariably arises when *people* are the conduit of the machine. Glover himself was the ideal candidate to lead this charge, and things may have lasted longer (though it was a wonder that they lasted as long as they did) had he remained alive.

Glover's original intention was always that his group of companies would lead by example, providing services and goods through automation while also using profits to sustain livelihood: a closed-loop economy based on a guaranteed minimum income that would showcase to others the benefits of such a paradigm and therefore self-replicate. Things began to change when the Glover Group elected its new board of directors. Decisions began to be made in which the Glover Group would acquire companies and administer them. At first, the Board's actions were public and positioned within a promise of integrity, that Earl Glover's generosity would be replicated by all the companies that were absorbed. Certain scholars argued that Glover's original intention to simply act as inspiration that would cause a cultural shift in the global economy was a more stable and sustainable model. However, citizens worldwide had already gained a taste of Glover's generosity, and wanted more—wanted it faster. Countries that had once been on the distant outskirts of the first world wanted to taste the salvation, and when the Board of the Glover Group promised rapid expansion of this program, the people, not the scholars, were quick to allow it.

The Board's transparency shifted into obscurity, and a critique of their decisions was replaced by blind trust. It was no longer clear which individuals sat on the Board, and the few remaining who paid mind to such things considered that the Board itself was a front, that it was possible that a single man pulled the strings, stacked the Board to work in their favor, and remained in obscurity orders of magnitude beneath oblivion. By the time the Glover Group's board decided to transition all the automation to clean energy, an epidemic of polluted air and sickness was already the new reality for much of the world. Even Glover, with all his planning, had not planned for that, blinded by his own generosity.

The Garden in Toko Valley

The Board was upset, but the Board was also full of dying old men — and the world was full of dying young men. I was hopeful but not entirely convinced that the meeting I was about to leave the country for would save my business. Certainly the Board of Vault Prosthetics saw it as some Hail Mary plea to an investor who would probably back out like all the others. But I was going to be staying at the Leidda Resort in Toko Valley, which made my staff a little jealous. If the business was about to implode at least I would get a spa pass out of it.

It was difficult to discern between the anxiety I felt knowing that I might lose my position if my company were to collapse, and the anxiety knowing that my company was in jeopardy of collapsing at all. I was attached to the Vault Institute and Clinic the same way I might be attached to a prosthetic, or to a partner I had spent a decade courting. In fact, if I were to trace back time to the origins of my enterprise, it would surpass any brief relationships I had.

Smog filled my lungs as I stepped from the car, my body heaving the entire way into the main clinic. Stephan, my assistant, looked up from his desk and hailed me over.

"You're not wearing your mask, Mr. Vault."

"I forgot it at home," I said to him, sitting down in the lobby to catch my breath and wait for the dizziness to pass. "Is everything ready?"

"I have your schedule cleared out for the next four days. Here are your boarding passes." There was a pause, his cadence signaling that he had more to say but was waiting for the right moment. "Also, Mr. Orsen is waiting for you in your office."

I told him to tell Orsen that he was in charge until I got back. I tucked the boarding passes into my coat, eyeing my closed office door behind which Orsen was surely ready to ambush me.

"He really wanted to talk to you," Stephan said.

Orsen was my Vice President and CFO, as well as my best friend. It didn't matter either way; I had no business with friends or employees. There wasn't anything to discuss until the end of the trip. Anything he had to say would be pointless until I secured the institutional support of one Dr. Rebecca Abra.

Stephan pulled a thick paper mask from his desk drawer and handed it to me. I held it to my mouth and left the clinic, glancing at the aluminum letters spelling out my name on the building and wondered if they would still be there when I returned.

I went home and smoked a cigarette, which was probably insensitive, all things considered, but I figured that having a synthetic lung meant I might as well hit it hard with the poison of my own choosing, rather than the poison of careless generations past.

I was going to turn on the news, but the weather was on. The weather was always on. The weather *was* the news, and when it wasn't, sickness was, and then they'd attribute it to the weather. And on and on it went, hours of nighttime newscasters hopelessly and frantically trying to pick out some shred of originality around the subject, never really letting the world come to terms with the situation, that they had been abandoned by their gods and idols for tokens and currency.

Orsen left a voicemail.

"Vault, you ass-hole, call me back." A heavy sigh came through the receiver. "What, you think because we're a month from shutting down that there isn't any work to do? Fuck!"

I could hear Stephan trying to wrench the phone out of his hands and Orsen's muffled shouting, "They're taking a fucking vacation in the middle of—*back off*— I'm getting a cold breath down my neck from the Board and a hot stick up my ass from the staff. Now I'm supposed to tell them all that the goddamn CEO is—"

I closed the phone and tossed it on my bed.

I packed a single canvas duffel bag with a few shirts, socks, underwear, and the two condoms that remained in the inside pocket from my last trip to Romania (which was not a business trip, for clarification). I left my computer, my business cards, and everything in my wallet besides what I would need to board a plane.

My first two nights visiting the Leidda Resort had been wholly uneventful. I spent most of the first in my hotel room reading up on Dr. Rebecca Abra, the woman I was to meet with on the fourth day, and her research on organ transplants. I had visited the bar, a sunk-in lounge at the center of a massive indoor pavilion and had little to drink in comparison to the other visitors, along with a small meal of beets, goat cheese, and candied walnuts all tossed into a salad that looked something like a sunrise of gold and deep red.

The bartender was a young man with dark hair and a thin strip of facial hair on his jawline, younger than me, seemed to enjoy his job, and he told me so.

"Pays the bills, and I get to spend my afternoons talking to people so rich they speak like they're from another planet. Can't beat that," he said. His accent might have been Swedish or Finnish but I couldn't really tell. He hid it well and spoke impeccable English.

He asked me what I did for a living. I told him I worked in the technology industry, which was true.

"You enjoy it?"

I told him that I did, which was not, not always anyway.

I spent most of those first days taking in the resort itself. I liken it a small city, with men and women bustling from hall to hall, thinking only of their objective, never really seeing one another. They all, like myself, were there for business, though I identified with none of them, the women or the men.

The Leidda resort was notorious for the crowd it attracted: politicians, heads of state, doctors, princes, *et cetera*. Then there was me, the kind of person who was invited, and had everything expensed on the backs of my company. I was not a rich person. Mild success had come my way, and respect in my field, but not much material wealth, not of this sort.

The striking thing about each person who passed by me was the *health*. People moved briskly, breathed without difficulty, and seemed eerily ageless. Money buys health too I suppose.

I fumbled with my inhaler, outwardly displaying a bit of shame, and waited until arriving at my room to take any of my medication, antibiotics for one cause, hormones for another.

I walked around the sides of the pavilion, where curving corridors of aluminum pillars and potted plants, skylights and tile slabs gave the impression of being both indoors and out. Not many of the guests I observed were stopping to look at the scenery, which was perhaps an indication of success for the designer trying to make the architecture fall away and be utterly void of distraction. It was not a place meant to bask in architecture (though it was an architectural marvel as far as I was concerned) but a space for business to be conducted in absolute comfort. I wouldn't call it a resort of excess, but as I took in the structure and details of the carefully curated environment I became vividly aware of how poor I was, at least in this context—like a tourist pretending to inhabit a space they have no business in, particularly in the eyes of those that do.

I wondered if Dr. Abra was the kind of person who had business conducted there often—if she was the type who belonged at a place like that. I knew how to interact with the super-rich; my former investors often were, though I doubt any of them have been to the Leidda Resort. I kept telling myself that it was all for the best, that the next phase in my career was about to begin. I was confident in this collaboration.

I had to be. Time was not on my side.

When I returned to the lobby, I observed five men huddled together. They stood close, facing each other and talking on their cell phones. It reminded me of how penguins huddle together, them in their tieless dark suits, and white collar shirts. The thought made me laugh a little, until one of the men looked up. I averted my eyes, trying to conceal the grin on my face. To my dismay, he tapped his phone, inserted it into his breast pocket and began walking toward me. The man had dark sunglasses, maybe, I wasn't paying much attention. He said my name, which surprised me. Even if he had worked for Dr. Abra and was waiting for me, I hadn't introduced myself to anyone other than the bartender. Of course, photos were easy to come by and my face is attached to a few engineering and medical articles on the web if we're only discussing the easy way, the free way.

I half-expected the man to tell me that Dr. Abra had cancelled our meeting, which upset my stomach a little, that she had decided my services weren't needed, my invitation to collaborate no longer of value, that I would have to settle for working with the *second* best expert on organ transplants in the world. I considered walking away before the man could speak any more, that I would just ignore him and show up at Abra's door anyway, her message undelivered, and therefore force her to honor our commitment. I just needed a chance to talk to her, to sell myself. People usually liked me when they got to know me, if I was perhaps underwhelming on paper. Of course, I'm not underwhelming on paper. I was as much of an expert as she, in some ways.

"You're the printer," the man said. I nodded.

I observed him staring at the shape of my slacks, then at my chest, then back down. I assured him that yes, it was real.

He removed his phone from his jacket, tapped the screen and put it to his ear, then walked off to join the penguin cell-phone huddle for another twenty seconds or so before they all simultaneously ended their calls and walked out of the resort together.

I went back to the bar that evening.

"Yeah, they come in from time to time," the bartender told me after I inquired. "They might work for Rebecca Abra. She's on the Leidda Resort's Board of Directors. I think they check in for her, or maybe they just come to look intimidating. They're around more often when Mr. Alice comes to visit. He built the place. They might work for him. They might not work for anybody."

Everyone works for somebody, I thought.

I told him about the exchange earlier that day, and he laughed when I mentioned that they looked like penguins. He had a nice laugh, and I could tell he knew exactly what I was talking about.

"So you're a printer?" he asked, putting a tall drink in front of me that I had not ordered, but enjoyed, and would not pay for that night. "Thought you said you worked in technology."

I explained that I was an engineer, that my name was James-Zoë Vault, and that my friends and my research team called me Zoë out of habit, and that my team worked on 3D printing, that we printed organs to be used as prosthetics for patients and those looking to extend their lifespan, the ones who could afford to have a heart that would never stop beating, or a inner-ear that would never deteriorate, told him we were weeks from shutting down.

"Sounds like you're making mechanical people, like in the movies, but I guess these days we need all the help we can get. My aunt died a few weeks ago. Simultaneous kidney and liver failure. She had lung cancer as well, which meant that surgery was risky since the chemotherapy wiped out her immune system and most of her strength. Not that she could have received a suitable kidney and liver in time." He poured me another drink and refused to take my tip when I offered it. "Do a lot of people get behind that? The whole fake organ thing, I mean. I guess if you can mass produce them then that's preferable to waiting for someone to die and hoping they are a compatible and registered donor. But I don't know how I feel about a machine inside my body keeping me alive."

Our bodies are machines themselves. At the microscopic level there were just parts accomplishing simple tasks with no knowledge of the greater machine they were a part of, no different than cogs in a clock, unperterbed by the meaning of time, yet intrinsically part of its measurement. Besides, there might have been a time when it was simply about waiting for someone to die and hoping they registered as an organ donor, but things are more complicated these days. One has to consider the blight of the outside world, and that virtually every living person has been affected by it. I didn't want to tell my friend behind the bar that even if his aunt had received a simultaneous liver kidney transplant, those organs were probably poisoned and therefore nothing but time bombs that would had made her death slower and more painful.

Yes, our bodies are nothing but machines, poorly made, and deteriorating.

His skepticism around the subject was common among many patients, but it always seemed to surprise me. It was true that for every adopter of synthetic organs there was another just as adverse to an 'inorganic' body, and while I'm fundamentally against stereotypes, the fact was that the vast majority of these folks were closed-minded religious bigots who would reject a fake organ that would save their lives just as quickly as they would reject a fake man who affects their lives in no way, but now we're getting personal. So they would go to people like Rebecca Abra, and get a *real* kidney, one that would wither and die just as fast as the last, if you had the privilege of finding one. But there are no waitlists for donors when you are in the circles of people like Dr. Abra, or for that matter anyone who does business at the Leidda Resort. She was an ally I needed to have, someone revered in the medical community, a household name if you followed modern medicine or just watched the news.

I had seen her in an interview once when I was in Berlin trying to get a small clinic off the ground for victims of terrorist bombings who had lost limbs. She spoke with charisma, charm, and authority, the inflections of her speech carrying the host and audience with her on a conversational campaign. The public adored her—and it wasn't just tabloids and medical newsletters that confirmed this; it was also the blogs and chatter going on about the web internationally. Abra had advocated for several world governments to make organ-donor registration mandatory. It was an incredible lobbying achievement, though nobody was quite sure how she did it. When I saw her speak though, it was clear that she knew how to sell an opinion, probably just as well as she knew how to transplant a brain, *which she had done.*

The world's first successful brain transplant put her into the public eye. Granted, it had only been a portion of the brain, but it was astounding all the same.

The recipient did not reject the partial brain, and, in-fact, exhibited no noticeable changes besides a temporary loss of motor skills which were corrected after about eighteen months of physical therapy.

I figured if she could get behind what I had to offer, she could convince anybody. I would be willing to sell her everything if she wanted. It wasn't really about the money—it was a little—but it was more about a young-lifetime of work being rejected time and again. It was about the stigma of synthesis, of the artificial, the *changed*.

I was a perfect example of something 'altered' in the eyes of much of the world. Humankind has come so far scientifically and yet we've somehow remained un-able to uproot ourselves from the foundational fear of something different than ourselves.

So many clinics and hospitals have refused to sub-scribe to our prosthetics, fewer still to our organs. Every deal at the last minute was always shut down. Investors would pull out just before term sheets were signed, med-ical journals would remove stories from print even after they had been written.

I couldn't understand why. Didn't people want to get better, to adapt to the changing climate, to rid them-selves of pain and suffering, to become abled where they had once been disabled? The more we were rejected, the more we were known for rejection. I felt shunned from the medical community. But Abra was my chance...

The bartender poured me a final drink and told me his name was Daniel, and I insisted he took the tip I offered, and he did at last, then casually slipped the bills into the front of his pants without breaking eye-contact with me.

He came up to my suite shortly thereafter and we had sex that night. It had been a while since I'd been with a man, and was, in some ways, my first time; in other ways it wasn't.

In the morning I dressed in my black suit, and when deciding between a black shirt or white I smiled and chose the black. It was, potentially, the proverbial funeral of my business after all. Mostly I didn't want to look like a penguin.

I packed my suitcase and kissed Daniel, who was still in bed, before leaving the suite. I left my key-card on the table the night before in case Daniel wanted to use the suite, which was booked out for one more night that I anticipated staying (Stephan does that when he books my trips, just in case) but he told me that he doesn't stay in the suites unless he has someone to stay with, which he usually does. I half expected him to tell me that the resort payed him to do those sort of things with the guests, and I think he half expected me to ask him so that he could tell me it was true. He told me to have a safe trip, and good luck at my meeting, and goodbye—using my preferred name, which we had discussed after I was sufficiently drunk but before we took the elevator up to my suite the night before. I told him the key-card was also a pass for the spa, and he smiled and nodded and waved me away.

A car was waiting for me out front, the penguin man drove the car out of the resort and down the private road leading to Toko Valley, where Abra's campus and research facility was located. I hadn't showered, which I regretted when a noticeable discomfort in my groin arose. The only thing which helped me feel somewhat clean was the car's cold leather upholstery.

The road wound through hills with nothing but green foliage on either side. The trees were blooming earlier and earlier each year, one of the few beautiful reminders of our changing, poisoned world. After twenty minutes on the road the penguin made a sound that wasn't a word but which indicated that we were about to arrive.

One final curve in the road and Abra's institute was in view, a circular multi-level complex of metal and glass reaching back to a two-decade-old design aesthetic that I still found pleasing. The complex was like a huge ring surrounding a central courtyard the size of a stadium. The car entered a tunnel lit by red LEDs at regular intervals and came out, seemingly too soon by some optical illusion or unnoticed acceleration, at the entrance of the campus, an open lot with metal arches towering overhead.

My door opened, and I was asked to go in and speak to the receptionist. I did so and was then escorted from one lobby to the next over the course of thirty minutes, ascending a number of floors each time. The art that hung in each lobby and hallway was both refreshing and distracting, all multicolored pastels lit from behind and sitting flush with the aluminum walls. Once I was on the third floor I was ushered by a woman in a lab coat who did not introduce herself but offered me a small bottle of water, which I accepted gratefully.

From within I could understand the structure of the building. Six rings: circular corridors cascaded out from the open center of the campus and nine floors stacked atop them. There were fifty-four discreet buildings, connected by enclosed exterior bridges. For each floor I climbed, I also came two layers closer to the center of the campus. The higher and deeper we went the fewer windows were present, and there was more backlit art on the walls, more tracks of lighting on the floors. We arrived at the top level of the inner-most ring and I had expected to see windows overlooking the central courtyard of the facility, but there were none, only a panel of frosted glass at the top of the wall running around the circular corridor to let in some natural light. The curvature of the building was more noticeable here in the inner-circle.

At the end of the hall was Dr. Abra's office, glass French doors let a blinding amount of daylight into the otherwise dim hallway. The woman in the lab coat opened the door for me and I entered.

Dr. Abra was just as I remembered her from her television interviews. She really does look just the same.

I realized instantly why the office was so bright. The ceiling was entirely made of glass, though the wall I knew to be overlooking the center of the complex was metal and windowless. It seemed strange to me that someone who liked natural light this much would keep the center ring of her complex so dark.

"Mr. Vault, welcome in. Please have a seat." I did as I was told then shook hands with Rebecca Abra.

I expressed my gratitude for her accepting my request to meet and offer my proposal. She raised a hand to stop me from going further.

"The answer is no," she said. "I have no intention of publicly promoting your printed organs."

My chest deflated, and I felt every detail of the chair, the arch in the arm rests, and my quivering arms upon them. My heart beat in my temples and the tenderness in my groin highlighted all the discomfort that cautious confidence had been concealing. Remaining professional, I asked her why she would have me come all this way if she did not want to form a partnership.

She smiled.

"The reason is that I *do* want to form a partnership. Just not the one you are intending. Listen, Mr. Vault, very carefully to me. This meeting is to facilitate two things: a request, and a demand."

I asked what the demand was.

"I want you to stop distributing your printed organs." When she saw the expression that came over my face she raised a hand again and continued. "It's nothing personal, I just can't have you doing it anymore. You've been setting up facilities all over the world and soliciting to hospitals and clinics. Rather than continuing to have my associates sabotage your dealings and buy up your property I thought it best to just talk to you personally."

I was dumbfounded. Six years of trying to build an infrastructure in which my organs could be accessible and affordable to healthcare providers, governments, private hospitals and clinics had ended in a fruitless hemorrhaging of resources. Now to find out that my last hope had in fact been the cause was enough to turn my stomach.

"Dr. Abra," I said, mouth dry. I took a sip of water. "I don't understand—"

"I know you came here seeking my help as a last resort for your effort, and I'm sorry I have to be the one both denying your request and funding your collapse simultaneously, but I think we can come to an agreement."

"With all due respect Doctor, tens of thousands of people die because of the lack of compatible organs for transplant. That has risen in the last eight years by over three-hundred percent. The way people take care of their bodies is different than it used to be, the climate alone makes up..."

I stopped when her eyes told me the information was irrelevant. I wasn't telling her anything she didn't already know so attempted a different approach.

"Now, here me out." I said, shifting tone. "You've made leaps and bounds with advocating for mandatory organ donor registration, but that just doesn't cut it, and those organs may fail anyway. There is a huge spread of infectious disease because of the escalated need for transplants and reduction in quality control. Pretty soon there won't be anything left. I'm trying to create a solution here."

"I understand, Mr. Vault, but let me address a few things you've said. First of all, no country on Earth has mandatory organ donor registration. Not one."

I hesitated, confused by her statement. There had been a massive export of donated organs from six countries. It had resulted in a booming economy for those nations and allowed for the rest of the world to keep up with the deterioration of health internationally. I had personally been to Germany, where people told me about how they were forced to register as organ donors.

Abra dismissively rubbed the corner of her eye. "They filled out the paperwork, yes, but we don't use those organs. As you say, there are too many risks, the spread of infectious disease being the least of them. We get organs here, you see. The countries that have instituted those policies don't actually use donations from their dead citizens. It just accounts for the boom in available organs and the vast reduction of those on the wait-lists. It allows the public to believe that their leaders are supporting a world-wide effort, and it costs those leaders very little to maintain that illusion. We do a good thing here, Mr. Vault," Dr. Abra said as sweetly as she did deliberately, "and you need to stop trying to solve problems that don't exist."

I stood so quickly that the chair fell backward. "How can you possibly say there isn't a problem?"

She frowned then. "Don't get so upset, Mr. Vault. I'm not your enemy here."

"Not my enemy? You've gone out of your way to wreck every effort I've made for the better half of my career!"

"You do good work too, Mr. Vault. I watched you when you first came on to the scene. It's great what you do for people. In fact..." She broke off and stood from her chair then began to unbutton her blouse. I was about to object but I noticed the thick and familiar scar that ran down the center of her chest, one that I had seen on numerous patients.

"A heart that never stops beating," she said, sighing almost ironically. "Remarkable, Mr. Vault."

She buttoned her blouse back up. "You see, I'm a customer, a grateful one, and there will be others soon. There are those looking to live longer, to move better, to transition more effectively, which is your specialty I believe. That is how I wish to partner with you. My associates would pay handsomely for that kind of service. They aren't interested in cheap organs for diabetics, or prosthetics for soldiers. They want the things you create that will give them immortality. Let *me* deal with the weak and the ill."

Unable to maintain eye contact, I looked down at her desk. There was an empty picture frame and blank sheets of paper along with an unmarked calendar. A couple of leather books had been placed strategically on the desk for decoration. This wasn't her office; it was just some pleasant meeting room, a place to feel comfortable, with its natural light and sensible decor. It made my stomach turn further.

I took another sip of water, lifted the chair and placed it back in its rightful place. "You can't possibly think that you can handle all the need that will come up over the next few years, can you? Once disease spreads enough there simply won't be enough healthy people left. I'm sure you've seen the projections. The demand will rise faster than any of us can account for. The entire medical community is in a state of panic."

Abra walked around from her desk and touched my shoulder. "The supply is here, Mr. Vault. That's why we created the demand."

"Created?"

"I think I've proven that I'm not against synthetics. Come with me, I want to show you something, in good faith, and to ease your concerns."

"What's that?"

She smiled. "I want to show you my garden."

We walked along the hall of the inner ring to the elevator, Abra's silence was that of emanating smugness, feeding off my confusion, her body upright and flowing like a restaurant host preparing to show you your table—performative. She placed her finger on a glass button and held it in place until a blue light flashed and went out, then the elevator began to move down.

Blue lights came through the vertical separation of the elevator doors, indicating every passing floor. I counted each one until we reached the ground level, and an amber-green light drew up the gap and filled the elevator as the doors opened.

I blinked once and saw a greenhouse, the sunlight filtered and reflected along the colored glass walls that made up the interior of the open space at the center of the complex. Greenery covered the ground, huge leaves six to eight feet tall, like an ant's view of a box garden. I blinked a second time, and focused my eyes in the light pouring down from above, realizing for the first time that the building was more of a hollow oval rather than a circle, and saw that there were not only leaves, not only stems, there were also pale green tubes attached to lanky stalks of the same color, each looked like a cross between a tree and wilting flower, with limbs hanging passively at the sides of the stalks. I blinked a third time, now with only a few seconds past and saw that the stalks were torsos, and the limbs were human limbs, and the plants were not plants, but people. Aisles and rows separated the 'crops' made up of three or four elongated sexless humans clustered together.

Abra's hand touched my back, and she led me forward down the central aisle.

The crops had no faces, though some had eyes, and all of them had narrow heads. They were all genderless at first, but as we went deeper I began to notice more feminine crops, with the illusion of hips and curved bellies.

"For ovaries and eggs," Abra said, "and perhaps soon, for surrogate gestation."

Every humanoid plant was legless. The thighs joined together where the knees would have been, and extended into round metal plates bolted to the ground. I felt knots in my stomach, and I turned to survey the garden once we reached its center. There were hundreds if not thousands of these human plants, so similar but with each cluster slightly different. I turned in circles and alternated looking at the ground, the walls of the institute, and the sky above.

"Shh. Listen carefully, Mr. Vault."

I stopped spinning and closed my eyes. To my left I heard a soft rhythmic sound, like fingers tapping on tables strewn about a room. I couldn't pinpoint the source, or imagine what it could have been, only that it reminded me of ticking clocks, but deeper.

Suddenly, I was brought back to one of my first research labs years ago, where the white sterile room fell silent the moment we assembled the printed parts of the first synthetic heart. Orsen was there with me, and we held hands and our breaths as the heart was attached to the pump and power. Grey fluid poured into it and a slight jolt of electricity followed by a steady current of power charged it. When it began to beat on its own we all cheered.

"The center is where we harvest the hearts," Abra said. "They require the most direct sunlight. But here. This is what I really want to show you."

At the foot of every crop with a beating heart a pulsating tube extended to a circular cobblestone dais, where tall green leaves concealed the smallest plant in the garden. Abra didn't have to tell me what was in there, I knew, but still I pulled the leaves aside, and looked at the small humanoid plant. Dimples and crevices gave it the features of a face, and the head, unlike the others, was full and round, while the limbs and torso were frail and shriveled.

"We only need one," Abra said. "She produces one brain every fourteen months. Even *you* can't print a human brain, Mr. Vault. So you understand why I need you to stop and focus on creating new and long lasting organs for my associates. Leave the organics to me, and I will heal the sick and the poor. I have thousands, Mr. Vault, and every blood type. Enough blood to fill a lake, enough eyes to count the stars, enough hearts to power a city." She smiled wide.

I asked her how long they lasted, and she told me that the kidneys would last for up to three years, the hearts for up to six if they come from the strongest harvest. Eyes deteriorate after eighteen months and require replacement, but they only take a few weeks to grow. Custom bases would need to be made for patients so that they could mount new eyes regularly without invasive surgery. That *I* would be needed to design and print such custom mounts.

I asked her how long she had been using them, and she told me a date, the first date one succeeded. The pilot plant simply produced blood, and blood was her primary source of income for many years, which helped fund her research.

I asked her who knew about it, and she told me her small surgical team, and her most generous investor, one Mr. Alice, the owner of the Leidda Resort. The owner of *many things*, she elaborated. On the southeast side of the garden was where she kept the patch dedicated for him.

I didn't ask to see it, but she showed me anyway.

She showed me the pale little bodies of children, the only plants that did not look like plants. The tube that came from the metal bases on the ground connected to their naval, like umbilical cords. They had eyelashes and lips, fingernails and feet, and they had genitals. They all looked like children between eight and twelve, boys and girls and otherwise. All of them pale, almost transparent.

"When Mr. Alice has them harvested," she explained, "they get a little more color. It happens when they begin to eat normal food. He is a good man, Mr. Alice. He is the reason you're here after all."

I asked why, not with my mouth, which was dry and quivering, but with my eyes, and she told me that he needed modifications to his body, and that I would be the one to do it, and that I would be receiving instructions when I arrived back at the Leidda Resort, and that I would be paid handsomely, and that I would go on to make more things, and that I would spend the rest of my life in luxury, and that I would spend the rest of my life looking over my shoulder if I ever thought of betraying his trust.

"One commission from Mr. Alice," Abra said, hailing me back into the elevator, "is worth the wealth described only in fantasy stories."

I drank the glass of water that was offered upon my return to the Leidda Resort, trying to subdue the nausea, thinking about things that were plain, in at attempt to cleanse my mental pallets, but I kept thinking of having sex with Daniel in my hotel room the night before, and how disgusting I found it presently, the organicism of it. I supposed I would never look at people the same way again, sexually or otherwise. I often found myself in sexual situations on work trips. But I also often found myself having a glass of water, or tipping a doorman, or riding in a car, or getting surprised by a response — and then the sexual encounter makes sense, because it's as simple, repetitive and mundane as the glass of water. But the sex made me want to vomit. Everything made me want to vomit. As the cars passed by, picking up and dropping off the patrons of the Leidda Resort, I thought about laying down in front of the tires of one of the limousines and letting it crush my head, so that neither my team nor Dr. Abra's would be able to rescue me. The doors of the limo I had been eyeing opened up and three men stepped out, wearing identical suits. They were the penguin men, and they no longer amused me. They shuffled over to me, remaining in close proximity to one another. I was handed a file folder that I did not open.

"Exact measurements for the request, and a complete health history of Mr. Alice. There is also a note from Dr. Abra. Your car will depart when you're ready."

I looked over at a white sedan that had just pulled up. A small girl with light blonde hair and the palest skin I had ever seen was ushered in. Another one of the penguins climbed in on the other side and drove the car away. I nodded and got into the limo, and when it was apparent that we travelled to the same destination as the sedan with the pale little plant girl inside, I was unsurprised, and then I finally vomited on the leather.

I send a brief but detailed email to Orsen, and then ignored his calls. On the fifth he left a voicemail.

"I'll notify the Board then."

The Castle in the Sea

I never really understood how it could be possible for something as trivial as a range of mountains to become such an incredible and influential facet of my attention and of my being, especially when I had not identified with them at all. I had become, quite unexpectedly, a slave to these rolling fixtures which haunted me, taunted me, and kept just out of sight enough to stimulate want for beauty but not so much as to allow the firmament to reveal its splendor to the eyes of the gazers and the wonderers and the wanderers, but this is trifling, and the digression strays from the point which I make which I strive for which is not important but which is that she was cold and things have changed.

I came down into the sea to be shown the castle at the bottom that we were told about. The one with the glistening spires and the glass walls, but the water was dark now and even if the trout would let you pass (and trout are preening and selfish creatures who won't tell you outright that you're dumber than them but will look at you with those eyes, invisibly blinking, and say as much as they'd wish to say and remain as dumb as they ought to be) the surface light stopped catching the glass a long time ago, and it's probably all clouded by now.

I remember once (and this was before the mines were on the land) we'd walk for miles her and I and get hopelessly lost in the greenery, (and remember that this was also before the mountain range was visible), and I thought she smiled once or twice at me, and she had good hair, and clean clothes and nice feet and we didn't really talk at all, but she was there and I was simpler, and the world was simpler, and she wasn't simple at all but I thought she was. We hummed little songs together when we weren't talking and we weren't walking and I don't remember what the tunes sounded like but they felt like hm hm-hm hm-hm hm hm-hm hm hm hm-hm-hm. Yes, that's right. That's what they sounded like.

I heard stories about the castle in the sea, and that if you stood too long in one place your feet would freeze underneath you, and so you had to keep moving, which wasn't difficult since you could swim and have no trouble at all, and the water was cool but it never bothered you, and the trout were friendlier then (that was before they got their spots) and their cousins, the koi, would come from a long way away to visit and they brought stories with them. I never got to hear those stories, the ones the koi told. I met a koi once, but he knew no stories, and didn't seem very interested, and suddenly he looked very much like a trout did and I left. But the stories were good, the ones I heard, and the ones that taught me things about who was who and what was what and where was where, but the wheres are different now. The sea is a little further off, and harder to get to and not as fresh, and the mountains are there now, and there aren't as many places to walk around and get lost in and still feel like you're on your way home. And the sea doesn't sing anymore. But I do remember that tune. How could I ever forget that? It went la—.

No, wait, that's not right. That's not it.

The Illusions of Acke Karlsson

They came in groups of two, lines of marching strangers entering the massive iron gates for the first and last time, they expected. Men with glowing electric sticks stood on either side, ready to attack any who dared break file, but none of them would, none ever did. The individuals in line entered through a set of doors into a grey building, a block in the valley, the palace of the Director of Development.

The Director sat atop a platform in great and profound darkness, while the board of secretaries sat in a row at a long table stretched across the great hall of Development.

"State your name, and your power, and the price."

A young girl was ushered forward, and she said, "Isadora Nicolascu. I catch fire. When I do my body burns away, and it hurts, and then I am renewed."

A murmur from the secretaries.

"And the cost of the renewal?" asked the Director of Development.

A murmur from those in line behind her.

"A shortening of my remaining lifespan by approximately 10%."

Silence.

"Demonstrate."

Then the girl looked around at the group forming around her, the double file line in which she had once stood feeding the hall's standby area behind her, and she closed her eyes. Her body shone somewhat, a pale yellow and then a deep red, and by the time it turned black she was hidden and engulfed in blinding flames. When she was finished, the flames died down and the vague outline of a corpse of scorched flesh stood in the darkness. The coal-black skin fell off in chunks to reveal the soft and supple flesh of a renewed body. She shook about, the burns cracking and drifting away in ash. She ran her fingers over her scalp and revealed hair, once again a vivid auburn that cascaded along her naked back.

She stood there and waited, knees shivering and pressed together, feeling the eyes of the Director, of the Board of Secretaries, and of the throng behind. A pile of her old ashy flesh and burned hair had collected at her feet. *It was her life, in that body*, she thought. Her life, gone and wasted, and for what? For a demonstration. She hated herself for it, for her willingness to give up her precious time, and wondered when it was that she would die at last. Would it be in flames? In her sleep? She did not know, and would never know. The body she stood in now felt foreign and strange, and although it responded as she expected, it felt borrowed. It *was* borrowed, from the cells that would have made up her body in some future months or years. The clothes she had entered in were gone now, but those were borrowed, and she felt no bond to them. She had been in those clothes only a few hours, but that ash around her had been her shelter for several years. She wondered how long it would be before she would have to burn away this new shell. Would it be to rid herself of some foul sickness? To scare away some attacker, or enemy soldier? Or would it be at the command of a higher authority? She found this last option to be the most unnerving, and also the most likely.

"Dismissed," said a member of the board, and Isadora Nicolascu was escorted away by the electro-stick wielding guards, paraded in her nudity through the crowed space and out of the hall.

Then there was a young man in his early twenties who came up to the circular altar before the Board and the Director.

"State your name, and your power, and the price," said the director.

"Thomas Renshaw. Shape-shifting. Agony."

"Dismissed."

Several others came up over the next several hours, with the same or similar statements, "Jack Carter, shape-shifting, agony. Mikael Biroozian, transmogrification, agony. Ajay Patel, morphing, paralysis."

Others would be asked to demonstrate, those who possessed unique traits, or if their description was unclear, or occasionally, if the Director became bored.

The crowd had been reduced by about two thirds, and the chamber smelled of burnt flesh still when a teenaged boy with pale blonde hair was called forward.

"State your name, and your power, and the price."

"Acke Karlsson. I can change the way the light moves, what is seen. The price is blindness."

"And so how do you know what the light is doing if you cannot see it yourself?" asked the director.

"I can feel it. I can hear it."

"And the cost of that?"

"I can feel it and hear it *everywhere and always*. There is no silence, and no peace, and no pain and no pleasure—only presence and the uncomfortable awareness of it, for even in the darkness, the light is there in small biting particles."

"*Demonstrate.*"

The boy opened his eyes, revealing that they were ice blue and glazed, and he smiled.

There was a ball then above the boy's head. It attracted the attention of everyone in the Great Hall of Development. Then the room was lit, and everything could be seen, including the Director of Development, and the Board of Secretaries. Though the Director looked like a slender man in a suit, the Board of Secretaries looked like monsters constructed of mud and tentacles holding clipboards and typing at laptops.

The director shielded his eyes and waved his arm in the air. "That's enough!"

But the boy did not stop. The room changed colors then, and they were not in the Great Hall of Development. They were in a grassy field surrounded by snow-capped mountains. In the distance, a marching storm of soldiers moved across the plains with electric flame machines and burned away the grass. Then they, the Director, the Board, the boy, and the group, were underwater, and there was a castle there, a strange and twisted version of the building in which they stood, the

Palace of the Director, but covered in undersea mold and barnacles.

"Enough!"

A school of angry fish chaotically shuffled themselves about, multiplying and swarming like bees until all the water had gone and oily scales slithered across every individual in the chamber. Though the boy could not see them, he knew that arms were flapping about frantically, and secretaries were gagging and holding their breath, their eyes telling their flesh what to feel, putting false pressure on their lungs.

Then the light changed, and everyone saw what had always been there. The men with the electric sticks charged at the boy and stuck the devices into his back. He convulsed, cried out, and fell to the ground all at the same time. Then they dragged him out of the hall.

He was deposited in a cell roughly two-hundred square feet large with six others around his age. A small barred window at the top of the cell let in the electric light of the sentry towers that illuminated the foggy air outside.

Isadora was there, still naked, sitting against a wall with her arms hugging her knees. A few of the others were shape-shifters, another pyrokinetic, and an immortal or two. Not all of them had been present to see what Acke did during his demonstration, but word travels fast when at least one or two individuals are able to broadcast telepathically.

"Why'd you do it?" whispered a voice in the cell to Acke. "They'll never let you out now."

Acke shook his head. "Of course they will."

"What makes you say that?"

He could feel all eyes on him, the little glistening bits of light that reflected from them, from the tears on Isadora's cheeks, they filled his ears and other senses.

"They're testing me, that's all. They're testing all of us. The way I see it—we've won."

Deflated chuckles from the other children echoed in the cell.

"Now I think you must be a little crazy. Are you sure that's not the cost of your gift? Delirium?"

"I've met Delirium, and this is not her," Acke replied, brushing the comment off. "Think about it—they kept me alive after what I did in the hall. Why?"

"He's got a point," a boy said. "I've heard the Director had a girl set on fire for breaking file and shouting out. No offense Isadora…"

The girl said nothing. Acke closed his eyes, listening, tasting, feeling the light that revealed to him the shape of her body, her bare flesh smoother than an infant's. He can sense every tremor, though the cell is not cold.

In a moment she was clothed in a white sleeved shirt and white trousers. She runs her hand across her arm and feels only flesh where she sees cloth and she knows it is an illusion, but she moves away from her spot on the wall.

"Thank you," she said.

"I could just make the guards think we've all disappeared. They chose not to isolate me. Why do you think they do this? They want to see if we're useful." He looks over to Isadora. "If any of us are useful, some of us, or none of us."

"So what do we do, Acke?"

"We wait—what else can we do?"

So they waited. To Acke, it was clear that only Isadora and himself were useful, that the others were being held for some other reason or perhaps to test Acke. They were being observed, he was sure of that, though by what means he couldn't be sure, a bug or possibly a camera. No, not a camera—he would have sensed that, the way they absorb light; it would have appeard to him as a gap, a hole, a void.

When it became clear that they would be waiting for some time until the test began, Acke began to formulate a series of events in his mind:

It was morning when the cell was opened, though only a few additional hours had passed.

The entire group was taken down a hall to the courtyard outside the palace of the Director of Development. The purpose was clear once they observed that a platform had been erected, on which the Director of Development and the Board of Secretaries sat looking down at them.

"They're going to make us fight one another," Acke said. He whispered so that only Isadora could hear his voice, "I'm sorry."

The illusion of her clothing vanished, and the light began to bend in new ways. The pyrokinetic boy made short work of the others when he thought that he was being attacked by a pack of wolves, and he burned himself alive when he thought that thousands of insects crawled across his skin.

Within seconds it was only Isadora, himself, and the charred remains of his former cellmates. Isadora stared at the dead youth, burned by his own power, knowing true empathy.

"Well…" said the Director of Development.

"I can't very well do anything to harm her, can I?" Acke said. "Besides, we're the ones you want right?"

The Director of Development made a gesture and the Board of Secretaries rose from their seats on the dais and slithered away. The Director led Acke and Isadora back into the palace. There were no guards flanking them, and no words spoken until they arrived in a lavish chamber within the palace. The door closed behind them, and the sound of locks echoed.

"So you figured it out," said the Director of Development.

"The demonstrations," Acke said, "they clearly had a purpose. If war is coming, then you're looking for specific traits that will be useful in what is to come. I can make short work of your enemies."

"And what," said the Director of Development in a slow and grainy voice, "would I need from *her*."

It was obvious, the way he had asked Isadora to demonstrate her gift when it had been so clear that it was useless in battle. His intentions confirmed themselves the moment he asked the question, he wanted Acke to be there, to say the words, to watch.

So Acke watched as the Director of Development removed his clips and medals, his belts and sashes, his decorations and uniform. He watched as the Director of development began to fondle Isadora's body, reveling in her new and infant flesh.

When Acke decided that it was a sufficient performance he lifted the veil on the Hall of Development, where the group of gifted youth were behind him, the guards with their electric sticks, and the Board of Secretaries at their long desk, and the Director of

Development standing naked in the center of the room, his hands grasping at nothing.

The Director of Development seemed to be the last to notice that the illusion had been lifted, that Acke had spent hours drawing the entire hall into a trick of the eyes, that they all had participated in watching a sort of play that they lost themselves in, none more so than the Director himself.

The Board of Secretaries stood from their table, looks of disgust on their faces as the Director of Development shriveled, words failing him as his mind scrambled for an explanation.

The Director of Development was dismissed by the Board of Secretaries then and there, and he removed himself from the palace that was no longer his.

The guards dropped their electric sticks, confused and without direction. The Board of Secretaries moved out of the hall single-file.

Acke looked to Isadora and the others who had been removed as they reentered the hall. He once again shifted the light so that Isadora would appear clothed, now in a uniform of red and grey, the colors some distant, obscured, or nonexistent rebellion—the colors of something other than their captors. They cheered and ran to Acke, embracing him and clapping his shoulders. They lifted him up into the air and paraded out of the hall, out of the Palace of Development, and out into the world.

The light shifted again.

It had been a nice thought, and his cellmates were utterly enthralled with the illusion. Only Acke was truly aware of where they were, the others so much blinder than he was. It was for the best, they would at least feel as though there was hope and goodness in the world before they died, that there was justice served to the wicked, and as the cell filled with gas, Acke smiled while he and the other rejected developments perished in a victorious delirium.

"We wait—what else can we do?"

And by the time the true illusion fell apart, they all had smiles glued to their faces, something the guards who came to remove them from their cell the morning after were never able to understand.

Daniel's Confession

I.

TO MY EXTENDED FAMILY,

I hope this letter finds you in good health. It has been several months since I last communicated with many of you. I am doing just fine and appreciate your inquiry. As I write, she is in the yard tending to the new cherry tree we recently installed. Oh, and what a tree it is! Full and lively scarcely describe it. Even then, on our wedding day she was eager to have me put a colorful tree in the yard. I remember that day well.

A December wedding, as many of you remember, those of you who made the trip to attend and were gracious enough not to let pettiness and formality sway your decision, was the choice of my wife. She has always loved the snow; it was the canvas of her imagination. She looked lovely that day and while she walked down the aisle I could scarcely breathe. My heart pounded hard in my chest as the knowledge that this beautiful woman would always be with me overcame me.

At the time I was an accountant, able to afford a modest townhouse overlooking the hills and I thank those of you who assisted us when we called, the two of you, at least—and to the rest of you: we hold you in nothing short of fond regard still.

She took such joy in decorating the front yard with spring flowers and ornaments to catch the sun. The back yard practically implored for us to plant a gorgeous cherry tree at its center. That tree was our only child. I know that many you had hoped we would have children early on, but it was not to be. We watched as the tree grew to become a remarkable specimen, a wonder. I confess that I have a few amateurish sketches of the pink blossoms tucked away in my desk drawer, though I would not ever let them see the light of day.

Yes, the house and the garden were lovely, but as I worked in my home office each day there was one thing that continuously caught my attention, a picture of my wife that hung on the wall opposite my desk, a photograph that captured the very essence of her beauty. Her smile gleamed in the morning sun and her eyes filled me with passion in the evening. This was all true of my wife in the very beginning, but is only so for the picture these later years. As the years went by my wife had grown weary, she still had a bright smile of course but her eyes became listless. Always more tired—I suppose that's what is to be expected when time works its cruelties.

Not for me. I stayed working with the same diligence as always, my vision never wavered, my ears and eyes never deceived me. Hers did.

The picture framing my wife's photo had begun to crack, and so I took the liberty to reframing it in a brilliant silver metal. This complemented the still vibrant photo. I found myself looking more and more deeply into the photo. It was the preservation of my sweet love. I no longer looked at the woman who shared my name with anything more than polite identity.

I stepped outside to pick up some of the fallen cherries in the yard and remained there on a patio stool in front of my office window facing the yard. Through the window I gazed into the photo while eating ripe cherries. The woman living with me questioned this and I told her not to bother me.

This woman harassed me to no extent: during times of labor and leisure. She asked for my affection, which I could not give. I moved her to a spare room upstairs; I wasn't quite sure why she had taken quarter in mine. After all, I was a married man. I still had a love for the woman I married, when I married her. She sat with me when I worked, and I spoke to her. She always remained quiet, sitting at the table, but I saw the love in her eyes. It was the love that she felt for me the day of our wedding. I gazed at her now for hours, her shining smile her glowing features surrounded in a silver frame, forever preserving her beauty.

This was the woman I loved. The woman I cherished. She is my only companion in the seclusion of these hills and I write to you to report that she is well and our marriage is a happy one, despite what any of you have thought or said to one another. I hold no resentment but would caution to you all that word travels quickly in this family.

The other woman who lives here, I expect she was brought to offset the mortgage, the reason escapes me now, I hastily send her off whenever she interrupts my time with my beautiful bride.

Most days I sit outside, eating cherries and chit chatting with my wife through the office window. She listens to me, every word I say. She does not interrupt or ask questions, and I think you all ought to take her fine behavior as a model for your own interactions. I have become somewhat of an insomniac. How can I take my eyes from her, after all? She hypnotizes me with her beauty; her long black hair flowing in the wind, in contrast to my greying beard—timeless. I feel myself aging now, time stealing me away from the world of the youthful. How could a vibrant young thing such as her ever have fallen for me? But it doesn't matter; she had, and has remained loyal to a fault. She sits there on my table, poised and pretty.

With affection and best wishes,

Daniel

P.S. Sending sweet cherries.

II.

Urgent:

I write in grief to report a crime. My happiness was taken from me. I had let myself fall asleep for an hour or so. The other woman must have been waiting for this, for when I awoke, my dear bride was gone! I found a silver picture frame on the sidewalk outside, the one my wife adored so much; she always had it with her. That other woman must have taken her from me. That hag! She was envious of my darling wife. I readily caught her around the throat with a necktie of mine and dragged her to the yard, making quick work of her and putting her in the ground.

She will bother me no more and justice has been served.

I send this letter to you all, my friends and family, her friends and family, some of you, both, if you consider yourself such. My dear beautiful wife, with her gleaming smile and wavy hair, is missing. I don't know what the wretch has done with her, but I have found no body. I still have a glimmer of hope that my wife is alive, and I ask you all to search for her, though I must confess, I fear that she is gone for good.

I ask this humbly after my long period of disassociation with you all—though I might mention that, should a few of you reflect, you may discover that you are not blameless in the cause of such estrangement. If she is truly gone then all I have to remember her by is the picture frame I bought for her, an anniversary present I believe it was. I feel her spirit shall always live on with the tree we raised, or at least under it.

With hope and anguish forever,

Daniel

P.S. Sending cherries. They are bitter.

The Affe(li)ction of Marco Martín

"The moon has a strange look tonight. Has she not a
strange look? She is like a mad woman,"

-Oscar Wilde, *Salome*

The splintered wood on the window sill catches his hand
as he makes his final successful effort to shut the bedroom window. Through the night he sleeps a few hours
atop the baby-blue comforter Abuela has constructed
for him, after which he will open the window so the
chorus of street noises, clicking insects and barking
dogs cures his insomnia. In the morning, he awakes to a
chilly breeze and the smell of potatoes and chorizo.

At some point Marco becomes aware that his feet
are not only dangling off the edge of the bed when he
wakes every morning, but that he has been kicking the
wooden frame. Tiny bruises covered the tops of his feet.

"You are getting too big for your bed, *mi hito*." Momma says when she notices.

He wears socks to the breakfast table after that.

★

He is happy that the bus is not full today, affording him the opportunity to sit alone on the way to school. The driver repeatedly tells him to sit properly in his chair but still he sits with his back to the window, knees at his chest. He feels the window rumbling with the movement of the bus over the road, and he relaxes his head against it, letting the glass softly pummel the back of his head.

Momma would not notice the tiny bruises that were forming.

★

The short nails on his fingers prove useless in attempting to pry out the most obstinate splinter of wood from the side of his palm.

In class he can sense Kyra eyeing him as his picks at it.

After school Kyra stops him and asked to look at his hand. He shows her, and she digs her nails into his skin.

He flinches, retracting his hand, but she smiles as she flicks the wood chip onto the ground.

"That hurt," he says watching blood pool in his hand.

She grabs his bleeding hand and opens her mouth over it, creating a seal with her lips. Marco feels her tongue prodding at the sore spot.

When he arrives home he instantly knows that Nana, Momma's abuela, is visiting, because she makes sweetbreads and never explains what kind of meat they really are. The smell fills the house.

Momma notices Marco's nails are getting long, reminds him to trim them, and Abuela remarks that his hair is getting long despite the fact that she took him to get it cut just one week prior. Abuela doesn't remember much these days. He scratches his thick black hair with his protruding nails, doubly confused.

He eats sweetbreads in tortillas blacked on the flame of the stove for dinner and enjoys though he does not know what kind of meat it is.

★

His dad visits, to Momma's dismay, every couple of months. She makes herself scarce whenever his truck pulls into the driveway.

"Don't mind her, *mi hito*," Abuela says, "she brings out the worst in him. Have a good visit."

They don't talk a lot. His dad mumbles, and most of the conversation is spent with Marco asking him to repeat himself or sitting in silence. His dad's hair is long and curly, pulled into a pony-tail and a loose braid. His arms are covered in tattoos. He chews on beef jerky, which he shares with Marco.

"Any girlfriends?" he asks. Marco shakes his head. "Good kid. Just don't bring your girlfriends to the house, your mother won't be nice."

His father leaves not long after.

At school the next day Kyra asks Marco if he wants to come over for dinner at her house.

★

Marco recognizes Mr. Kapur from the open house at the beginning of the school year. He is friendly and speaks clearly unlike Marco's dad, despite his accent.

The meat Mrs. Kapur cooks is unlike any Marco has had. It is not spiced, and is prepared to a wellness that, upon being cut, oozes a bloody redness. Kyra tells him that it is lamb.

★

Marco's feet kick his bed frame in a rhythm matching the sound of the running paws that fill his dream. He hears snarling and sees a family of sheep out in a field. The smallest lamb falls behind the flock as he approaches. In a moment, he is flying through the air and descending upon the lamb. The taste of blood fills his mouth, unpleasantly, but then becomes meat, he imagines the flavor of dirty pennies becoming sweetbreads.

Blood has pooled on Marco's pillow, the inside of his cheek inexplicably raw.

Momma notices the way he chews his potatoes and chorizo, avoiding with some difficulty one half of his mouth.

"Just a toothache," he tells her.

She looks at Abuela, and they remain silent. Marco has never been to a dentist, and is glad he doesn't really have a toothache since there is no way he will be going to one anytime soon.

"It's okay, it doesn't hurt much. It'll be better tomorrow."

The next day is a painful breakfast as potatoes rub against his raw cheek. But Momma notices and smiles.

★

"I'll show you mine if you show me yours."

The first time new skin is revealed is the first time Marco became aware of his capacity to turn, though he did not fully.

They slipped off their socks and put their feet together. Marco winced as Kyra prods the now large singular bruises on the top of his feet.

She runs her hands up Marco's legs and flinches when he lets out something not unlike a whimper or quiet bark.

"I'm sorry," he stammers, "I don't know what that was."

★

Momma notices Marco walking with Kyra.

"Who's your friend, huh?" she asks.

"That's just Kyra. She's in my class."

Abuela enters the room and knocks over a picture frame.

Abuela is only clumsy when Momma is about to get mad, and only to distract her.

Marco goes to bed.

★

They walk in the rain, and though Marco enjoys the cold, the flecks of water bother him, the little bits that land near his eyes, the dampness becoming wetness.

"When it's raining," Kyra says, "I like to imagine I'm underwater, what it must be like to live like a fish."

*

They were teenaged lovers, and she has long since become used to Marco's shifting. He learned not to sink his claws into her, and how to compose himself as he turned.

It is under the stands of the traveling circus that they discover that Kyra could bite down deep into his flesh and he would not turn. It is the first time they have sex, the first time they could. Marco's mind was rife with passion and confusion, the wolf in him stampeding through his blood and howling behind his eardrums.

*

Momma tells Marco that his father passed away that night. Marco is numb to it, understanding only that he is now among the ranks of boys without fathers, but not knowing how to feel about it either way. He hopes that Momma will finally tell him what happened between them but doubts it.

"I know you weren't close to him, but he's still your father."

Something about the situation emboldens him, and later that night at dinner he asks Momma, "Did you love Dad?"

Abuela looks at Momma, imposing a warning.

Momma looks down at her posole and then aside.

"I did love him. But only half of him loved me."

That night, Marco confronts the wolf in his dreams, he imagines Kyra standing between him and the huge grey thing. Alone, Marco sees her as the girl he has grown up with, told his secrets to. The wolf licks its jowls and hums deep in its core. Kyra faces the wolf and lets her skirt drop to her ankles. Marco feels no passion, but the wolf laps at her flesh with its tongue.

He can hear Abuela's voice, "she brings out the worst in him.

"*Ella saca lo peor de él.*

"*Ella saca el lobo en él.*"

★

Marco and Kyra break up months after the circus.

Gabriel and Marco have been seeing one another more and more. When Gabriel's fingers weave into his, Marco has no inclination to turn. The wolf is silent and still, and Marco is filled with nervous passion. For the first time, his legs and stomach quiver, and they are his own, and his cheeks are not torn by sharpening teeth when Gabriel's lips press against his.

"It's not that I don't care for you, but I'm not the half who loves you," Marco says to Kyra.

"You'll be happy with him," Kyra replies, a smile on her face failing to distract from her watering eyes. She wraps one arm around him and presses herself against his body. She kisses him, lets her tongue slide across his long sharp canines, and finally bites down on his lip and sucks it hard.

Gabriel and Marco hold hands in hallways, and Momma and abuela take to him quickly. Abuela always tries to feed him when he comes over, and she calls him his 'good friend' even though she knows they are more than that. Marco reminds Gabriel to just smile and agree, and to eat or she'll just keep asking.

Every couple of weeks Kyra and Marco call on one another, and Marco allows his affliction to take hold of him so that it can be forgotten in his life with Gabriel. It is the only way the wolf will grant him any peace. Kyra will lick the blood from her lips afterward. Her affection fades as Marco's body returns to that of a boy's.

She calls it his *affeliction*, some perverse marriage of affliction and affection. The thing that loves her and is a disease to Marco.

Gabriel calls it that as well, though he never says it aloud to Marco. He never brings up the scars that appear on Marco's skin after he has had a night with Kyra, but he knows. Momma notices the scars, and follows Marco around with a cut stem of aloe vera until he succumbs and allow her to dab the succulent's juice onto the bite-marks.

Abuela eventually buys Marco a larger bed for his room, one where his feet do not hang over at night, and one that he can share with Gabriel, and, on occasion, with Kyra.

Great Fall

Dedicated to Traci Turner

There was a time when the ground was destroyed, and every living thing began to fall.

Many died at first, as fear and shock overcame them. Some did not. They grew accustom to the endless falling. Walls of rock on either side, a chasm of infinite depth was all they knew. They hunted other falling beasts. Nature continued in a freely moving environment. Children were conceived and were born with the sensation of falling familiar and comforting.

And so the story goes.

Eventually, after generations, an evolution began to take place out of necessity. Hands and toes and limbs became webbed and outstretched to facilitate easier movement in the air. Eyes developed a film to resist drying out in the ever-flowing wind. Bones became brittle, as there was no need to support joints and movements of the past, the lean muscles would become the protector and the support. Ears became cone-shaped to shield the lateral sounds of the falling plane from the rushing air. Changes went unnoticed taking centuries to occur, and by the time one change was completed there was not one left without such an adaptation.

The endlessness was of no consequence to them. At first, the fallers thought they were moving to some destination far below, but after such a long time, the abyss became entity without meaning. It became their sky. Their God.

A stranger evolution began to take a number of the fallers, and their webbed limbs became wing-like, their nails more like talons. This generation wholly disregarded such changes, making no use of them, until one broke form.

He suspected that there would one day be an end to the chasm, and that all life would fall to its death, and this frightened him.

Driven with fear and gifted with wisdom, he used his evolutionary gifts to stop falling. First, by breaking the taboo of making contact with the earthy walls of the dive. He used his talons to grip into the dirt and scraped down its length to slow the descent and eventually stop. Many terrified and confused faces looked at him, but quickly vanished far above, or to him, deep below. All life left him behind, clinging to the wall. When he gained the courage, he leapt off and began to fly. The wind and air filled the length of his fleshy wings as he flapped away his limbs, muscles strong. The next logical evolutionary step had been taken. He flew upwards, and for the first time in all of known history, he was ascending. He was, in a way, moving back in time, to a place long since left behind. But the air was there, and was the same, and there were patterns in the walls that were familiar to him from younger days.

Though he became tired, he would not sleep and fall as he had his entire life. He continued to ascend, taking only short breaks to clutch the walls of the chasm. He looked about, seeing that the walls ran parallel to one another, each a visible distance from the other. But beyond that, the walls extended endlessly upwards and endlessly outwards, though gravity still pulled down— or what some of the fallers came to call up. He would sometimes lose his way and let himself drop a bit to reestablish the direction he wished to travel.

A great amount of time passed for the one who ascended, but at length, he caught a glimpse of something different. In the distance was another who had dared to ascend. She stared at him with stark surprise.

At that moment, a sickening sound filled the chasm. The sound was heard for an eternal distance, a kind of quiver in the walls followed the cacophony, the sound of crashing, of millions of bodies coming in contact with a ground they had been accelerating towards for ages. The ascenders looked below but saw nothing. At last it had occurred; the end of the fall had come. There were no screams, there was no time, for they collided in their sleep. Even the beasts had no time to howl.

There was no turning back. The couple continued to fly upwards. One carried the other while they rested, then switched, finding that this allowed them to climb faster than ever before, and knowing what the fall meant gave them motivation even though the climb was still a mystery. When their children were born and eventually strong enough to make the climb themselves they were more adept at flying that either of their parents.

In time, the ascending parents died, and they fell again into the chasm below. The children, however, had come to know the ascent as the only way to live, and that falling meant death. They had been told stories of the falling people, and how they came to their demise. They shed no tears as their parents vanished from sight, for the climb was their life.

Across the vast space of the chasm, others like the first ascenders had sprouted wings and flew upwards, had heard the end of the fall as millions of souls crashed to the end, and their children were the climbers now. They found each other, and formed groups. Their children could fly faster and longer without resting against the walls. Their ancestors had fallen to their demise, but new generations of fliers came. When one grew old and weak, they would fall, and join those before them, and the rest would honor them in song. In the end, they would all end up at the bottom, but the climb continued.

The time of the fallers was reversing, and every space they had fallen through was now passed by an ascender who had long forgotten that the fallers were their ancestors. To them, the first climbers were the beginning of life, and the fallers only legend.

And so the story goes.

The third way of life, as the ascenders called it, began when one day they reached a ledge.

The top of the chasm had been reached, and a new life began.

Over time, their wings disappeared and other traits evolved, those needed for the life on ground.

The the fallers were all but forgotten. The climbers became a distant memory, then legend. The walkers were all life now. They kept a peculiar ritual from the past. When one died, they would group together, singing an ancient song, and toss the body into the chasm, where they believed the realm of the dead to be.

But life went on, until a later time, when the ground gave way again, and the walkers began to fall.

The Precise Place of Hail Counterpart

Hail took his laptop out one day, an expensive machine that he used to write things in and do other work. He was a writer, and a man who loved gadgets and things very much. He would keep his fingertips very dry and free of lotion and wash his hands often to prevent smudges and fingerprints from getting on the clean aluminum casing on his devices. His laptop was regularly cleaned with a microfiber cloth and the keys were polished, and the device was protected by rubber case. His almost obsessive care for the device made it strange that he would be sitting in such a misty place to write.

Truthfully, he had actually spent all day looking for a miserable misty park. He *wanted* to be in a place with mist, and it didn't seem to bother him at all that the dampness was collecting on the surface of his laptop, it didn't matter; this was the perfect place, and he had spent a rather long time trying to find it.

He had seen it in his mind, and just knew that on that particular day, it was the ideal place to sit and write what needed to be written, and since he had no other responsibilities, nowhere to be on a Sunday, no one to see, he took on the mission of locating this place in his head which would be perfect to write what needed to be written. There had to be a place just like it. It is only a park, after all. He wanted to be in a park, but one that didn't give off the aura of a poor romantic comedy that he had just seen, one gloomy enough to be inspirational but just pleasant enough to have life, and perhaps a few families about with their children or dogs but was also quiet.

The issue was the mist. The place he had imagined was misty; that is to say, there was fog, but not a thick fog, just an opaque and nebulous haze that would chill the air pleasantly around him, and kiss his skin with subtle dampness without making him sweat from humidity, but would still be cool and wet.

Several hours had passed when he found the place, at which time he uttered the word 'precisely' and smiled and opened his laptop and began to write in the place he had imagined to be the perfect space to write.

He was a writer, a writer of emails. Emails containing a number of things from appointment reminders for him and others, to notices, or agendas, or sometimes he would write things to fire people, to out people, to warn people, to threaten people, to direct people.

He wrote an email to his supervisor, and quit his job, and then crawled under the bench and went to sleep, leaving his machine above him to collect moisture.

The Infatuation of Jaime Coin

They said my mother would have been a genius, except that only sixty percent of her blood was reaching her brain. So she was mildly absentminded, "a total blonde," some would say. But growing up, I would see these moments of brilliance and insight, where she would read people and their emotions, make precise calculations, and act. I chalked it up to instinct, street smarts as my sister called them, but when I found a picture of her as a little girl I knew. She has that same look as I did, piercing and insightful, pondering and calculating. Her eyes looked beyond the lens of the old Polaroid and read me, I could tell, even through a forty-year-old photograph.

In the market, people would look at me as a baby and say that I looked like my mother until my dad came by. I looked like him, the spitting image, but he is no genius. I saw that look when she was a child and knew my resemblance to be truly hers, and I had complete blood flow. I could execute absolutely those things which my mother could not.

I met a girl in college. She was brilliant, and creative, perhaps not wise but that was probably for the best. I was happy to have someone in my life with whom I could have an intelligent conversation, and everything seemed as if it was the first time. The first time I kissed her was like kissing my high school sweetheart. I knew this because I had a high school sweetheart, for a few months, but she was dull and normal, much to my dismay. The similarity was the newness. I had partners of the body, but a partner of the mind was far harder come by, for any person or creature could sympathize with aroused genitals and intimate contact—far fewer could appreciate a conversation as an equally sexual encounter. Her words and ideas made me want to be with her so much more than her body would have had she not had a mind of her own. But she also had a body that I could be infatuated with. I loved that girl; I loved her in a way I had never loved before.

There were others. Girls and boys who I could say I loved, but never had the pleasure of a relationship. She was the first, in so many ways, that I could hold and touch and kiss, and I adored her mind and her body, I loved her whole being, where before I had compromised one trait for another. She was everything to me, my strange and pragmatic, almost sociopathic, self.

To be loved truly by a sociopath—I wished for her sake that I did not love her. I felt guilt for bringing her into my life. But I had also felt guilty for the others whom I did not love but said I did. I felt guilty for her because she was everything, and I did not deserve her.

Is this what real people feel?

My mother's friends would come to my mother for advice, and I was a fly on the wall for each encounter. They would speak openly, thinking that a child so young could not understand. But I was my mother's child, and looking back I think she knew but did not care that I took everything in, because she knew the value of understanding reality. She was insightful and would absorb their dismay, filter it, and place before them a catalogue of uplifting dialogue, comforting empathy, and a prescription of next steps, all of which seemed to place her in a powerful position. It was a masterful approach to social engineering, and she was the one whose genius was crippled. She only got as far as a mediocre job and only vaguely legal activities. I used the gift to persuade senators and students, masters of the universe, bureaucrats and chiefs.

To be clear, sociopaths can't love, if we're to have a technical debate about it, to deal in absolutes.

The thing I admired most in my mother was her *handwriting*. She could be so unrefined, blind and also be so proper, and understanding. She is not what one would call book-smart, but she has a lot of world experience, and in that case, is more brilliant that I will ever be. It would be like pulling teeth though, trying to get her interested in something I liked, to get her involved, and explain it in a way that would allow me to have an intelligent conversation with her on a subject. I never could. But it isn't entirely her fault, since the things I was interested in were not simple. It made it hard to talk to her about the books I read, and the plays I watched, and the music I listened to. But god damn when she picked up a pen in her left hand and wrote, I think I could weep. I could read the stunning and perfect cursive all day and night. I could stare at it for hours. If she were to write a transcription of a novel for me to read it would be, regardless of the story, the greatest reading experience of my life. The way the capital letters soared above the others in her signature, a swift and elegant simple three-stroke character that set the stage for the tiny and deliberate letters that followed, resembling a mountain on the horizon of a inked identity. A paragraph looked like a letter you'd see in false writing to make it look like an old-fashioned script, but you could *read* this. I remember lying on the floor with her in the closet when I wanted to hide and she would come to find me and I was just learning to write in cursive and I would practice in the carpet. She lay with me there and corrected me when I stopped the stroke to cross a 't' instead of finishing the word and going back to make the crosses and dots. I always tried to copy her signature, and it shows in my own, though they look nothing alike, the strokes are similar in the capital letters and I think of my mother's whenever I sign my name. Almost every single time.

This was the case when I affixed my signature, in ink if not in blood, to the contract which bound me to my new post. Everything would be left behind now. The girl from college couldn't quite understand to where I had disappeared, and my mother has long since passed. Though she may not have made it this far, it's her hand that is now filed in the records of the Board of the Glover Group. I will take my place soon among the ranks of the most powerful men on the planet, at a company founded by a man I've admired my entire professional career.

The rest washes away. The love, and the frustrations. The work is everything now.

Stones

I used to watch my father hold the stone high, the sun's rays bronzing his skin. And he held mine for many years. When I was strong enough I held my own and I admired my father's strength. He told me stories that his father told him.

I found, one day, a string and used it to hold my stone up. My father was saddened. He said that nobody would ever hold their own stone again, that I would not know the reward of holding it up myself.

I used my time to collect more stones, sat atop them and gazed up at the sun, and listened to his stories.

My son emulated me. But he took the extra stones and stacked them and built towers around him.

I was saddened that he would never know the feeling of the sun's radiance. I told him the stories my father told me, the best I could remember, and sometimes I would embellish here or there.

His son, my grandson, spent his time inside of the shelter, writing stories on stones. And my son was saddened that he would not know what remembering was, or notice the subtle ways the stories changed depending on if he told them, or I told them, or my father told them, or his son would repeat back to him.

I will never know how to strive for the infinite knowledge, and my father would be sad that I still do not hold up a stone, but that's okay for him. To be honest, I'll never know why he did it in the first place. I think he would be proud of all the stories that have been collected, if a bit disappointed about how pale we've become.

The Shame of Alistair Fletcher

It was a curious thing, finding myself in the room which was not empty nor full, large nor small, finite nor infinite. It was white, by all accounts, despite the sort of wave of shapelessness giving the impression of depth—or perhaps it was simply filled with light, and there was a girl who sat across from me with her back against some invisible wall, knees tucked up against her naked body, face down and hidden between her legs, her long wavy hair mixed with streaks of chestnut and blond. She did not seem to be crying, but was obviously scared, obviously awake, and quite obviously aware of my presence. Had she been there before me, or had we arrived together? What involved 'arrival' at all?

Her head did not rise, did not make eye contact with me since we had existed in this place. The details of our 'arrival' were a mystery. I could not recall the events leading up to being in the strange white room with this naked girl across from me, and I imagine she felt the same—only more vulnerable (I was fully dressed in the suit that I had worn that day (what day?)).

That day. How long had it been? I couldn't remember a time when I was not in this room, like an eternal present surrounded me. It was always *now* and every moment of *then* was simply an abstraction of the *now* which was **forever**. The present did not yield to the future in the way to which I was accustom in the other world, and the girl eternally buried her face into her knees and I eternally stared at her, pondering my situation. It was eternal until something *changed*, until one of us moved, or *changed*, or acted; and so I *changed*, breaking eternity itself. I stopped thinking about why I was there, or *that* there I was. I thought of the girl across from me, close and incomprehensively distant at the same time—out of reach of course, but with every detail visible, every vein of her feet and ridge of her knuckles and strand of hair. I thought about it, that I could have her if I wanted. She was small, and exposed, and quite beautiful.

I thought about having her forever, but forever proved too long for her to remain hidden and eventually she fell asleep. Her body stretched out across the floor and her slumber was deep. I could see her breasts now, small and round, and I could see the light blonde trail of pubic hair which moved down into the shadowy crease between her crossed legs.

She woke up after a few quiet eternities and I realized that I had been staring at her the entire time. At this point we had both lived a thousand lives together, alone doing nothing, and she no longer had shame in her nudity. She had slept it away, and I bore it then, the shame, in every waking moment.

I suddenly got the sense that I would be missing an important meeting.

The Adoption of Addison Grace

My name is Jack Orsen, and I am probably considered by a ton of people to be a monster. At least, they might call me that if they knew me, knew the circles I was a part of, knew the things that I've done. And most people don't know a goddamn thing about a goddamn thing. But there's still some shit that basically all documented and accounted for by one or two people, and now, I guess, by you.

It wasn't until the threshold of some arbitrary inhumanity was crossed, into those circles, that I had any sense of time or space at all. I had gone through life ignorant of those things which I once called injustices or horrors, true perspective out of my reach. Those circles do not exist on the edges, where the light touches the darkness, but rather above the surface world, casting a darkness that the creatures below mistake for light. Circles of power, of desire, void of morality—if there is even such a thing. I sure as hell don't know if there is morality anymore.

They were told not to cry, or scream or whine—their word, not mine. Still, they were children, and they did cry sometimes—and it would shake me to the core and I would go months if not a year without doing it again. But the itch would turn to a burning, and I would get over it, whatever shock or remorse had welled up within me. I never really forgot the sounds of the crying, they simply faded enough for me to distract myself, and pretend, in those fleeting moments of perversion, that they did not exist.

There's something that happens when you have that much money; you enter a different world, a world of parties and drugs that were practically fables when I entered the workforce, a world of waste, a world of sex, and you never realize how far away you are from the law until a police commissioner shows up to have a line with you, or an officer pulls your car over for speeding, takes one look at the underage girl in the backseat and just nods his head and drives off. You become immune to the laws of countries who believe in laws, having that much money.

How much you ask? I own a penthouse with sixteen rooms, and that's just my New York location. I own similar spaces in every major city in America and others in Stockholm, London, and Moscow. Then there are various lodgings prepared for me in every populated region in the Northern Hemisphere. The sponsorship of a certain Mr. A— and my place on the Board of the Glover Group secured this lifestyle. I am rich by association only.

There was another, a friend of mine, good friend, and he was the one who pulled me into the circle. We were sitting at a bar in Stockholm, one of those modern jobs with multicolored ceiling lights and sunk-in lounges, all black and white and leather and vapor.

He could see I was uncomfortable, a little apprehensive, but he lured me in all the same. So much of what has happened is a blur, softened with drink or removed entirely by any substance you could get your hands on for $10,000 an ounce.

He talked to me as we drank.

"In ancient China," he said, "the emperor was considered so sacred that the people could not even look upon him. Think about that. Here, look at my hands. A typical acquaintanceship does not require you to have any attention to the way my hands look. But here they are, every detail, every unique quality. Now, if you saw my cock, how different would it be? Just a cock. Mostly the same, but the fact that it's *my* cock, with its subtleties and differences, that's something else entirely. In the workplace it would be obscene for any of us not to wear shoes, to see your boss's feet, but at the poolside retreat it was an appropriate setting, and everyone took the opportunity to look at my feet, get a glance at something forbidden, a curiosity only because it is hidden when the sun is up.

"So you see, it's not about the sexuality of it at all. It's about how *sacred* we make another's body, and that *sanctity*" he says this really slowly, savoring the consonants, "becomes visceral and passionate and eventually a lust for release.

"I don't give a fuck about cocks, or feet, or hands. But I crave every detail that makes them yours…"

He took my hand in both of his, raised it to his mouth and drew my forefinger between his lips, across his tongue, and into his throat.

We'd been friends for a long time, but he never did anything like that before, never. He'd been in too long, an associate of Mr. A——, as distant as I am now, but that's enough. Four or five degrees of separation from him was enough, as forbidden a sight as the emperor. The only thing I regret that night is being forthcoming to him, telling him what I wanted—desired. He told me he could make things happen.

Yeah, shit happened. I didn't really do much, just asked for things, ridiculous things, and they would come. Money cascaded from my words, my commands were worth more than I had ever made in the clinic. It only got bad when I started asking for the things I *desired*. Want and desire are different things.

Getting what you want does things to be people. You spend a long time growing up learning to set realistic expectations on what you can have in this world, but fuck, when you can have everything, when there are no more boundaries, when you uncover those deep and dormant parts of your mind that you've been shamefully hiding away for a lifetime, then it gets really fucked up.

So yeah, they were told not to cry, but they did sometimes. I never had to say anything, it was like the staff (the swarm of men in black suits who catered to me) were so in-tune with my mood and my patterns that I would be sitting in one of my apartments naked and jerking off on a couch so expensive your ass doesn't stick to the leather and one of the staff members would open the door and bring me someone. Scared the shit out of me the first time, but after that I came to expect it.

They could tell what I wanted, who I wanted, and by the time I had grown accustomed to my lifestyle, they had it down to a science. But I can't blame them—that's no good. It's me. It's always been me, I own that. I'm the one who can't just fuck adults like a civilized human being, they're just the envoys of desire, professionals.

There was one though. When they brought her to me I hadn't been expecting it. I definitely wasn't in the mood, but I got the sense that they knew that I'd be interested.

It was a fair assumption. She was perfect, everything-in-the-world-that-pleased-me incarnate. I won't describe her, she's my daughter now, I adopted her. No lie. Never touched her once, but I'm not looking at it like I should be applauded or anything. Truth be told adopting her was probably more fucked up than anything else I've done.

She had come in, and she was trained. Probably entered the trafficking ring when she was two, everything was practiced. She would know exactly how to behave, how to shift her eyes in pleasant delight when cued, to act impressed or passive or any other combination à propos of the client in mind. My one solace is that when you have as much money as I do you can be assured that she had never had to perform for anyone, that no hand had ever touched her. So, when she came in and dropped the thin sheer cloth that had wrapped around her body in such a performative way, all I could do was walk into one of the rooms in the apartment I had never set foot in and lock the door behind me, leaving her alone and confused.

In the morning, I saw her there sleeping on the couch, wrapped in a blanket. I walked over to the front entrance of the apartment and knocked on it. One of the suited men was waiting out in the hall with a small suitcase of girl's clothes. *They always knew.*

I left the suitcase open on the couch near her head, then walked to the bedroom that I actually used, showered, and changed into a fresh suit. She was dressed and sitting upright on the couch when I emerged.

"What's your name?" I asked, and she told me.

I held her hand as we walked across the busy city streets and stopped for breakfast at a café on the corner.

This little ritual was one we repeated on a daily basis, always at the same place, ordering the same thing besides the days when I drank coffee, which wasn't often.

One morning the two of us sat together. It had been a number of months after the adoption, and she had taken to me. Maybe she thought that all she had been trained to do was just keep me company, and that everything was meant to be that way. I found that much more relieving than the alternative, which was that she knew exactly what she was prepared to undergo, and was simply waiting for it to happen, not fully understanding the timeline of such things. How was she supposed to know that I would normally have the others sent off the same night after I was finished with them. Of course, this assumes too little of her. She had bright intelligent eyes that took in everything around her, and while we sat in the café, those eyes locked onto something just as mine did. We both saw him at the exact same moment.

He was beautiful, probably only a year or two older than my girl, Addison. The boy triggered something in her, and I wondered what she had been through to have such desire triggered in her, a girl so young. I knew at a moment what he triggered in me, and I was reminded of the circles I was in, of the suited men who were always watching me. I immediately averted my eyes and clinked my fork and plate to distract Addison.

Thankfully, the boy's parents ordered food and drink to-go and departed shortly thereafter.

"Do you want to talk about it?" I asked Addison Grace. She just shook her head.

I loved that girl. I loved her like I think my father loved me, but I'm not convinced. I guess I could call it a father's love, maybe not.

It was less than a week when I heard the front door creak open. Addison was sitting on the couch and I was in the kitchen making some kind of drink, hot chocolate or strawberry milk or something like that. I knew that when the door opened in that way it was my suited assistants delivering to me one of their procurements, a sort that they have not delivered to me since Addison Grace walked through my door.

It was the boy from the café.

I eyed the suited man in the doorway who ushered the boy in.

"What did you do?" I asked. But he said nothing and stepped back into the hall, closing the door behind him.

Less than a week. I knew what that meant. It meant that this boy was not conditioned the way the others had been, that took months. His parents were dead now, I knew that much. Whatever they had done to him to keep him so calm, so still, I didn't want to think about. He took a few more steps into the room.

I glanced over to Addison, her eyes wide and fixed on the boy. She stood from the couch and walked toward him. The boy remained motionless.

Something came over my Addison then, something about the way she tipped her head. I had seen it before, the gestures of a trained girl. She looked at the boy the way the others had looked at me and seeing from the outside paralyzed me. It was like watching a train wreck in slow motion. I couldn't stop it, I couldn't move. Perhaps I didn't want it to. I watched her do things to that boy, all the things she had been trained to do with me.

I wanted out, out of the circles, away from the suited men who sensed my every whim and acted upon it. I didn't want this. I wished that the children in front of me weren't there, had never experienced whatever ordeal the suited men of Mr. A— had put them through. I wanted them to disappear.

Just as the thought entered my mind, as if on command, the door opened again. The large hands of the suited man wrapped around the necks of the boy and my Addison Grace. Then there was silence.

At once, all the energy that had paralyzed me erupted at once. I screamed out loud, "Fuck! Fuck, what did you do!?" I collapsed on the ground wringing my hands together and slamming my head, knuckles, and knees against the tile, as if trying to break the ground beneath me. I heard the door shut, and by the time I stopped shaking and climbed to my feet, it was as if there had been nobody there at all. They were erased.

I don't go to that property anymore. In fact, I can't remember which state or which country it was in. I'd know it if I saw it. The white carpet and furniture would be stained with red wine and shattered glass would litter the floor. My screams would most likely still be resonating in the halls.

The drivers know not to take me there anymore, wherever it is. They always know.

The Patient Caretaker of Mars

She was a *wonder* to behold, perfection incarnate, though she was only a tiny sliver of the Tree of Life — a branch if not a twig. Her eyes shone, and at her most real and true moments, when she stared into me, when the sky was painted dark pastels and the sun was hugging the horizon ready to set for months on end, when her mind was attentive only to me, her fingers would spread and grow and blossom into purple glowing orbs, into orchid bouquets to mast her face and her toes would become roots and displace the cool earthy sod, and her skin would be pale and her skin would be bronze and her skin would be ebony like her mother the tree, and I loved her so much, and I would not touch her in her perfection but elect only to stare at my privileged singular view of that radiant demi-divinity and she would reach out to caress my face and the bark that had been fingertips moments before would scratch me gently, and she would unearth herself and become something so fickle, all flesh and passions and distractions and while we made love I wished so much for her to be less of a creature and more of a tree again.

★ ★ ★

It's going to be a long solstice. This winter will be endless and cold. The Tree of Life scorns her icy imprisonment beneath my feet, and she will wear another icy blanket this winter. I bid farewell to the sun.

★ ★ ★

There was one instance when she became something so feral and inspiring, the first time I think, and the moment I fell in love with her—I *worshiped* her as her fleshy body mounted me and kissed me with her hips and breasts and at the knees and elbows she was wood and her hands and feet burrowed into the grass that sprouted wherever she stepped and I was pinned down and trapped in a cage of her body and at the mercy of her unyielding focus, her eyes a rare shade of gold that they have never been since, and I worshipped her, and I would have stayed there forever beneath her, under the shade of her hair and the orchid blossoms, and I think it is the nature of the creatures of nature that they run and hide and find something different after you are their conquest, but she knew at that moment that I was the only living soul on the planet's southern surface, and so her face did not show disappointment—but once the gold in her eyes faded, she became content, a state within which these creatures are not meant to exist.

★ ★ ★

I am the caretaker of the tree. I am a failure, for I am trapped with dilemma. To melt the great caps of ice and free the Tree of Life would also free the toxic air and suffocate me. But the tree would breathe the toxins, make the air pure and fresh, make this world a living place again so my race's goal would be complete. But in my death the tree would have no caretaker, and would surely wither. I think it would surely wither. I know *I* would wither long before. I am afraid to die alone, and the idea of the tree dying is what keeps me atop the ice, and ignoring the tree below, so great and so full of life, preserved and dormant, but alive, and I will stay alive so long as the tree is alive and my charge remains incomplete.

★ ★ ★

She learned, out of necessity, out of boredom, to love me, although she could have run away sooner, obeyed her nature, mighty twig that she was, she stayed, I supposed out of the greater nature that we shared, a fear of loneliness, and she was a lonely branch of a branch of a branch which was the first and last and only to peek out from the ice when the tree was growing still, this nymph, and she came to me, knowing I was to care for her, though truly we both knew she took care of me far more, and possibly would have loved me the way I loved her if she was capable of it, of seeing me as more than a source of affection and caretaking, more than a play-thing to work her charms upon, more than some servant of man's expansion, servant to her mother, as well as imprisoner of her mother, for my reluctance to free the tree from the ice below made me the ice as well, or worse perhaps.

It is no wonder that she was reluctant when I asked her to do the thing that would save the tree, and save myself, for what spirit creature like her would resign her body to an eternity bound to some earthly thing like myself?

★ ★ ★

She has been away now for a year, I think. Although the days on this world are only minutes longer, the year is nearly double, but I will wait here, ageless as the tree deep below the ice allows until her daughter returns to me once she has tasted her spirited freedom and will finally wrap me in her flesh, and will encase me in her bark, and will breathe for me when I free the tree below and let the poison free and for years and eons I will care for the Tree of Life and the surface of this world will change and then, perhaps, after a short eternity she will be free again, and then there will come many more like me for her to play with. *This* is how I know she will be back once she is ready, because her nature is unyielding. She is the perfect creation of nature, and will become something she is *not* because it is her only hope of creating a world where she can once again become something she is and ought to be.

I am fine with being a small part of that.

The Complications of Nils Glass

Nils Glass pulled his coat's collar tight against his neck and observed the faint haze of his breath drifting off into the cold air of the winter night. He admired the quality of the suit he wore and the leather coat over that, and even took moments to regard the fine stitching of his dark brown gloves. He could think of nothing else.

Distractions.

The coat seemed foreign—where had he purchased it? Had it been during the trip to Paris he had taken with his wife the year before? Or was it simply a mistake, one made by his assistant, Penny, or by the dry-cleaners where she picked up his clothes?

You're stalling, Nils.

He enjoyed the cold very much, or rather, he enjoyed being warm while in contact with the cold. The winter calmed him—the silence, and there was no wind, the ideal night to be standing just outside of the hospital.

The courtyard was mostly empty and poorly lit. A solitary light descended into night from a floor high above, where a curtain was left opened in a room.

Keep standing out in the cold and you'll be a patient here instead of just a visitor.

There was someone speaking to him, but he was not interested in other people. He was reminded of that which he lacked, and that was decisiveness. He had managed to avoid making major and minor decisions for decades, so it seemed like his predicament was a cruel irony written by a vengeful god.

He entered the hospital, anxiety attacking him as his looming decision drew nearer both temporally and physically.

When the time came for making choices he deferred to others or would simply say 'I don't care' and hope somebody with a stronger opinion than his own would allow the situation to get on. His life had often come to a halt leading to arguments about his inability to decide. He felt the eyes over his shoulder just out of sight. People noticed his flaw, and this displeased him, but he had no right to be displeased.

It's my own fault really. Makes sense that they're pissed.

He got into the elevator, squeezing past an incredibly large woman in a wheelchair who smelled of oranges. He liked oranges, but this still annoyed him. He was not a rude person, but many things annoyed him when there was a decision to be made. His mind was at a standstill and his body wanted to keep momentum.

Momentum was lost because of things like elevators and heavy women and now the nurse blocking the door to room 6012. She greeted him as she had every day for the last three months, but he did not hear her words—the repetition had made him numb, like taking the same trip to work every day and never really reading the signs flying past.

Nils had not worked in three months. He showed up every day—but being indecisive, frustrated, and working at an ad agency makes for a somewhat unproductive environment. He would delegate final decisions to his interns, making his job more about soliciting students than generating ad campaigns. Punching the clock and doing no work made him feel hollow, but everything had gone wrong, and as Nils stepped into the hospital room each day, he was reminded of how wrong it was.

Displeasure took form on his face, tightened corners on his lips. His fingers tapped rapidly on his thighs. It was practiced and automatic, and as utterly unnoticeable as the fine stitching on his coat that was not his probably.

He stepped in and sat in the chair beside the comatose body in the hospital bed.

Nils Glass was responsible for making a decision. "She's not displaying much brain activity," the doctors would say. "End the cruelty and let go," the woman's family would say. But Nils Glass was only interested in what *she* had to say. He waited for her to break the silence in the cold sterilized hospital room, but she did not speak.

She did breathe, albeit artificially. Her chest moved up and down, and, under the sheets, it looked almost natural. Almost.

And her breaths pleased him, the irritating smell of oranges forgotten. It made him feel that she was alive, although he knew that she was not. He wanted her breathing to continue nonetheless, because that was what was happening, the present, a reality not decided by himself, and that would remain unchanged forever if he wanted.

"She's a lovely woman."

The voice that spoke in the empty room was a man's voice that Nils Glass was certain spoke English in his ears, but could not put an accent on it, nor could he recall the exact tone of the words once they were said. He could only recall that the words were spoken slowly, uncomfortably, and were accompanied with the sound of clicking jawbones.

The words were there again. "She's a *lovely* woman."

"She's my wife," Nils Glass responded to the nothingness.

Yes, he thought, *I will be a patient soon*. He thought this hopefully, for the insane were exempt from responsibility, mostly. All his decisions would be made for him if he were insane, and so it was perfectly okay by him that he was talking to a voice that was in his head.

But it was *not* in his head. It was beside him.

He turned in his chair and looked at the figure sitting in the corner, in a seat that had not been there before. The figure, at a glance, was a hooded shadow in the loose form of a body. In time, it actually looked like a kind of living skeleton, but with thick man-sized limbs that looked as if there were muscles and veins and fat underneath a layer of ivory bone. He could not see the figure's face, only perceive it from over its own shoulder, like a body just out of the frame of a camera.

"Your wife, yes. Lovely," said the figure again, and the bones clicked. "Her name is…"

"Linda," Nils said, "no, wait—it's Sam. She hated being called Linda. Her name is Sam."

The figure said nothing, and though Nils was looking at his wife, he knew that it was still sitting there, and felt its eyes on him. He did not mind the company, whether it was actually there or not. It didn't matter. He only wished it would say more—*prove* to him that he was, in fact, mentally ill. Things would be easier then.

"I don't want to make the decision," Nils Glass said, half to himself, and half to the skeletal man in the corner.

The figure made a humming sound. Then it asked him if he would ever kill a man, and he told the figure that he hadn't really thought about it much, but he supposed he could and, in fact, would if prompted to do so and if the circumstances were correct and the consequences would be limited. Then the figure told him that the consequences would be minimal, and to him, be immaterial, and that he—the figure—could relieve Nils of his burdens.

"I make your decisions *for* you. Hm?"

"That sounds nice," Nils Glass responded. "Is that going to cost me anything?"

"You do what I decide, and then you don't have to choose anything at all. Maybe at one point you decide to take the reins, and that's fine by me."

Nils Glass thought this was a simple thing, enough at least to distract him from the bigger responsibilities, and so he said, "Okay."

The hooded figure stepped towards him and into the light, leaving its shadow behind, and taking the image of a business-suited mass of bones.

I.

The bone-man in the black suit patted Nils Glass on the shoulder, moved to the door, and beckoned Nils to follow. Out of the hospital room, down the stairs and out onto the street they went. Nils followed the bone-man without question. He didn't know why. He didn't really have a good reason not to, and he had agreed, hadn't he?

The coat is suede, Nils thinks. He wouldn't have purchased it. Sam didn't like suede. He did, but he never shopped alone. He was the mannequin for her to impress her style upon.

Maybe I can bring Penny shopping. Speaking of shops...

"Here," said the bone-man.

Nils peered through a storefront window, past some indoor potted plants to a shop within, containing an impossibly diverse collection of antique home decor merchandise, much of which were smaller than picture frames. Besides picture frames themselves: there were glass and wooden figurines of cats and birds and horses and such, and bowls, and hooks, and paintings of frogs, decorative gyroscopes and globes, plastic gnomes, and a mobile of stained glass. Nils spied a single customer perusing the trinkets, and far at the back was a bespectacled little man coughing into a handkerchief behind the counter. In front of the man was a cash register and a sign that read, 'ALL SALES ARE FINAL. NO REFUNDS.'

The customer, a woman who carried a massive purse and had huge silver hoops in her ears (Nils was immediately reminded of the orange-smelling-elevator-woman) had been fingering a sort of lawn flag and was on the verge of knocking over a display of the glass mobile, which upon finding the flag was not to her liking, she did, in fact, knock over. Even from the outside he could hear the stained-glass shatter and erupt into a cloud of dust, daggers of translucent colors scattering all about the floor. The woman craned her neck, looking around, and when it was clear that the man behind the counter, who looked not entirely ancient but had certainly been young a very long time ago, did not notice the crash, or even jump at the noise, shuffled out of the store without saying a word. Nils moved to gesture to the man from the other side of the window, to tell him what had happened, but the hooded man placed hand on his shoulder.

"Leave it be," the bone-man uttered, and Nils watched the woman disappear around the corner.

"Come on, let's go inside."

Nils and the bone-man entered the shop, and only Nils worked to avoid stepping on the great unnoticed mess. He realized that his view of the counter was obstructed by the shelving now. From the layout of the store it was clear that the old shopkeeper could not have seen the woman knocking over the mobile.

"Must be deaf, or close," Nils muttered. He could hear the little man coughing more intensely. There was a shuffling of feet, and the sound of a door opening and closing at the back. The bone-man led him to the counter, the old man having stepped out. Nils inspected the area surrounding the old cash register which had a fine layer of dust on it with the exception of the numeric keys. Three of the numbers were worn away more than the others, '6' '4' and '9'. He looked at the prices of things on the walls. Most of them were tagged

$4.99, or $6.99. On the counter beside the register was a coffee mug which steamed with a foul smelling citrus tea, which caused Nils to clench his jaw. Beside the mug was a small orange prescription bottle, half empty. The sound of the man's coughing from the back room roared, the man approaching the door.

"Take them," said the bone-man, indicating the white-capped container.

"Beg your pardon?" said Nils.

"The tea, and the bottle."

Nils paused for a moment, and felt compelled to object, but the man's word was absolute, and he did as he was told. He took the hot mug in one hand and raised up the little amber bottle with the other, inspecting the label which read ETHAMBUTOL among other things in small type.

The little man reentered and looked at Nils lifting the mug and bottle just as the bone-man said to him, "Let's go. This way."

He looked at the little old man and followed obediently through the rainbow of stained glass debris the crunch of it under his feet. The man was trying to protest but had instead entered again into a fit of coughing.

The bone-man held the door open for Nils, the door closed behind them with a chime that had not sounded when they entered. He glanced back through the glass door as the shopkeeper, handkerchief pressed against his mouth slipped and fell into the shards of glass. Nils looked at the bone-man, imploring to let him enter the shop again, but the head shook from left to right, and the sound of bones cracking gave him a sickly feeling. He could only look back at the old man through the glass. The handkerchief was now soiled with blood either from his cut, wrinkled hands or from his lungs expelling, Nils couldn't tell which. The man struggled between getting to his feet, controlling the involuntary convulsions of his bleeding glottis, and reaching out a hand of pleading toward the window, to Nils, who had to stand there and watch him die. And he did die, eventually. Nils was sure, though he never reentered the shop to inspect the still body. The whole situation filled his being, and he was sure.

"Why did he have to die?" asked Nils Glass.

"It's complicated," the bones clicked, and the man looked more like a living shadow now, his black suit shifting between fabric and black smoke cascading over thick and unnatural limbs gilded in ivory.

"Well that's no good! People don't deserve to go like that."

"How does a stranger you have never met *deserve* to go then? Let's hear you decide that."

Nils was silent.

"Life and death are filled with complications," the figure declared, "but in the end, they are made of simple things."

The darkness and the bones moved onward, and Nils Glass followed it down the sidewalk.

II.

Love is eternal
You never stop loving someone.
But over time love is tempered with other emotions,
like hate.
　　And that makes things complicated.

They came to a clearing at the center of a vast and vibrant park. Trees sprouted up from the rich green sod at regular intervals and a cool breeze shifted the leaves and produced a gentle hum. A wooden bench at the end of the opening was a perfect view of the entire park. The bone-man sat on it, and Nils took a seat beside him.

"What do you see?" said the rattling jawbone.

Nils looked about. "I see the trees, the grass. I see the sun."

"No," it clicked in a low and deliberate tone, "you do not."

"That's right," Nils responded, looking around puzzled. "I see the moon. How long have we been sitting here?"

"What else do you see?"

He looked out into the clearing. There was a young man standing by himself, dressed in black clothes that were loose on his thin body, torn, but not out of poverty, out of some perverse choice of style. There was a beanie on his head. Nils could see in the darkness that he held a white paper bag, and he rolled and crunched it nervously in hand.

"Who is he?" Nils asked, but did not receive a response.

After a few moments the young man was joined by three others in similar attire. They would ask questions, and he would give them the paper bag, and he would ask questions, and they would shout, and he would turn and run, and they would shoot him in the back, three shots, and he would fall down into the grass, then the other boys would go away.

Nils wanted to ask why the man brought him to this place to watch this happen. Then he thought, *had* he known this was going to happen? Or was it a coincidence? The bone-man had already risen and was walking toward the abandoned corpse. Nils got up and followed.

In the darkness, he could not see the blood coming from the body's back, but he knew it was there. The bone-man, almost invisible in the moonlight, instructed him to search the corpse's pockets, and Nils did as instructed. He found a wallet, but it was mostly empty save for a business card with EXOTIC TOPLESS GIRLS — BAR AND LOUNGE printed on it and a crumpled picture of some ad agency logo. There was a pocket knife, which he did not open, as it made him uncomfortable, and two condom wrappers, one of which had already been ripped open and emptied, while the other, attached at the perforated edge, remained intact.

Nils looked up at the suit-clad bones expectantly.

"Check his waist."

Nils placed two fingers into the space between the young man's belt loops and his boxers and ran along the circumference of his waist until he felt the steel object that had been stored there. He pulled a gun out and held it. It was the first time he had ever held a gun, but it didn't make him nearly as uncomfortable as the knife had. He secretly hoped the bone-man would not make him take the knife too.

"Is this what we came for?" he asked though he knew it was, so they walked from the park. As they passed the last set of trees, he thought out loud, "What do you suppose they shot him for?"

"Life and death are filled with complications, but in the end, they are made of simple things."

"Yeah, you said that before. I get the cryptic thing but it's getting a little irritating."

The bone-man stopped and said, "You don't have the right to be irritated."

Nils regarded the bones and swallowed, mouth suddenly dry. "Sorry. Yes, you're right."

"You're pathetic, Nils Glass."

Nils said nothing and contained a festering rage that eventually became a solemn confirmation.

III.

It was daytime again, and though Nils Glass couldn't remember the night, he did not feel tired or disoriented. The bone-man and he were sitting in a diner, which was mostly empty in the hours following breakfast but not quite lunch yet. A young waitress whose name badge read 'Penny', served them. The figure didn't order anything, and while the girl had acknowledged at the beginning that there were two of them at the table, "Any coffee for the two of you?" she had said with a smile, she had not made any point to make direct conversation with the quasi-skeletal figure across the table from Nils.

He ordered black coffee, and the ivory-bone-covered face did not, and the girl walked away and disappeared into a metal door behind the bar.

"Sex," said the bone-man.

"Excuse me?"

"With her," it articulated, jerking its head towards the door the waitress had disappeared behind.

"What?" a drip of coffee dribbled down Nils's chin. "That's ridiculous! I'm *married*, and Sam wouldn't..." but as he spoke he found the futility in his words.

He had fucked other girls before, but only once since Sam had gone into the hospital and became comatose. It was his old friend, Angela, who had gone to girl's school with Sam, and that's how Nils met her. Nils hadn't pursued it, but Angela had been forward once his wife was in a coma. He couldn't decide whether it was wrong or not, and in the meantime, the affair had already started.

The thought of sex with the waitress was absurd. Nils didn't consider himself overly attractive, nor did he consider himself unattractive, but this girl couldn't have been older than seventeen, and he had been married for a decade. He could have been her father, a young father, granted, but it wasn't far off.

She did say she looked up to me. When did she say that?

"I look up to you, Mr. Glass. This is my dream job."

"Waitressing is your dream job?"

The girl had returned and was looking as Nils, perplexed.

"I just asked if you were ready to order?"

"Right."

Shit, I'm hallucinating. Probably lead in this old diner paint. Place looks a little like the set for the Cola ad last year.

"French toast please," Nils said, confident as this was the only breakfast he ever ordered, opting never to peruse a menu, particularly one with several pages, and the girl smiled and walked away, ignoring the bone-man altogether.

He looked into the skeletal face across from him.

"Can I ask, are you dead?"

The bone-man looked out the window, and then back at him. "I am not dead, no."

"Sorry, you just look…"

"I look like this. That is the way of things."

Nils shifted in his seat. "Ever had French toast?"

"No," the bones uttered.

"It's Linda, erm, Sam's favorite. You should try it sometime."

He made a curious look, though his fleshless face both moved and remained still, not entirely like a skull and not entirely like a face. "Perhaps I will, one day." It seemed as though the figure was searching for something else to say, but resolved only to, "Thanks."

"So, about this whole thing. How does it solve my problem? What about Sam?"

"You're not ready for her yet. Give it more time."

Nils nodded. "Guess so. Sorry for the questions, this is just a lot to take in." But it wasn't really a lot to take in. It was all very simple. "So this *does* lead up to Sam. That makes sense. I get the whole learn-a-lesson-by-following-the-strange-apparition-guide deal."

The waitress returned with Nils's French toast, said, "I'll be right over there if you need anything, sir."

"Grab me a coffee, you know the way I like it, Penny."

The girl winked, "You haven't touched the one in front of you." She went off.

"May I," the bone-man paused and loosened the tie around his neck, "ask *you* a question?"

Nils was genuinely surprised and swallowed the first bit of syrup soaked toast. "Yeah, of course, if you like."

"Why does your wife Linda prefer to be called Sam?"

"You mean you don't know?"

The head shook, and the bones cracked again, but it was softer now. "Why would I know that?"

"Oh, well I figured you just knew everything. Um, well it's a complicated story. See, she was adopted, and her parents named her Linda. Open adoption, but the birth parents didn't stay in contact or anything. She really hated the name Linda, and so she visited her birth mother when she was about seventeen. It was the first time they had met, and Linda asked what she would have named her if her mother had kept her."

"And she said Sam."

"No, actually. She said Wynonna if you can believe that. Of course, the woman was a little high at the time too."

For a moment, Nils thought he might have seen a flicker of something in the hooded man's hollow eyes, and swore he heard something akin to a chuckle. It was almost human.

"Do you want a bite?" Nils asked.

The figure looked down at the plate and said nothing.

"Really, I'm not even hungry. Here," Nils said, and unwrapped a clean fork from the banded napkin on the table and stuck it into the French toast, then pushed the plate over. The bone-man took a moment, the darkness dripping from his suit in odious tendrils falling over the booth. Finally, and with a degree of hesitation, it picked up the fork, cut off a corner of the toast and slipped it past its teeth.

"Well?"

"It's…delicious."

"Anyway, Sam asked her birth mother who her father was. She told her it was a guy named Redge who lived across town. She went and saw him. Successful guy, married, with a little girl, nice house too. It was obvious that he didn't know who she was, and she didn't want to start trouble, so she told him she was conducting a survey and just made up questions on the spot. Sometime during the conversation, she found out the daughter's name was Samantha, or maybe she overheard the wife say something in the background. I can't remember exactly what it was. I don't know if it was just a choice, that she liked the name, or that she somehow wished that she had grown up in a place like that. Either way, she's gone by Samantha, or Sam, ever since."

"You keep calling her Linda."

"What's that?"

"In the hospital, and just now, you called her Linda both times, then corrected yourself."

Nils nodded. "Yeah I guess I did. She's been in and out of the hospital for about a year now, and even before the coma she couldn't do or say much. I've been talking with the doctors and nurses, calling credit card companies, the cable, that sort of thing. Sam used to do all of that, and everything is in her legal name, so I've been referring to her as Linda for a while now. Plus, there's the mail that is all addressed to Linda Glass, and then the medical charts and documents. The hospital staff give out birthday cards to the patients, and Sam got one a few months ago. It said Linda on the front, and I haven't had the heart to correct them. I didn't know if it was even worth it."

"I see," said the bone-man.

The waitress returned with the check. "I'm going to run in the back real fast and I'll be right out to get that. Can I take your plate?" Nils looked down and realized that his companion had completely finished the French toast.

"Oh, yes please."

She picked up the plate, winked at him and vanished into the back again.

"It's time," said the hooded figure.

"Really? Are you sure?" he asked, and the bone-man nodded. "Is someone going to die again?" A second nod.

Nils got up from the table and walked behind the bar counter and pushed the metal door open. To the right was the kitchen, and to the left was a collection of sinks and dishes piling up. He recognized his plate. Around the corner was a large door that looked like it might have been a produce refrigerator. It was open, and the waitress was there inside. She turned and looked at him, startled at first, but then smiled and looked down at her feet. She peered around the corner to make sure nobody was around, and then looked at Nils. He walked toward her, into the refrigerator and shut the door behind him.

"Hello, Penny."

The girl opened her mouth to speak, but he already had his lips against hers. Her young lips were smooth and warm, and her mouth tasted like mint chewing gum. She did not resist, and when that became clear he took to her white blouse and pulled it hard in both directions until the buttons began to break and the top opened wide. Without removing his tongue from hers, he pressed against her and pushed her back against the cold shelves. Nils firmly grasped the crease between her legs. The girl began to rock back and forth against his hand. He lifted her onto the shelf, displacing a number of red and green peppers, a couple tubs of tomato ketchup, and a jar of paper-clips.

His fingers moved across her skin. He did not undress himself, just unlatched his pants, hers came off next, and contact was made. He braced himself on the shelf expecting to feel cold metal, but instead feeling suede with fine stitching under the girl's legs, his jacket that was not his jacket.

He used his arms to hold her in place, and while he was not exactly strong, the girl was small, and he felt stronger than he had ever felt in his life. He felt powerful—*decisive*. The world around him spun.

Penny broke the kiss and cried out in some mixture of pleasure and pain, gasping for air, but continuing to rock her hips with his, moisture pouring from within her. The impending climax was building within Nils, he took one final look at the girl's curveless form and the gun was against her head. It was impossible to tell if he had finished before or after her death, but to him, the orgasm and the sound of the bullet penetrating the girl's skull were one in the same. The feeling of her cold sweat and her splattering blood were the same. He stared at the look of fear plastered upon her face, a mixture of realization of the gun being raised and her own orgasm happening simultaneously. He withdrew, letting her body go limp and fall across the shelf. The sound of the shot being fired reverberated about the metal space but was contained within it.

He shut the refrigerator behind him and walked back out to the diner, the gun in his hand. The boneman stood there, nodded and said, "Life and death are filled with complications, but in the end, they are made of simple things."

"That wasn't complicated," Nils said.

"Exactly."

"Was that your decision? Or was it mine?"

The figure said nothing, and they left the diner.

IV.

Things that are difficult are often associated
  with things that are complicated.
But there is no correlation.
  Hard decisions are simple ones.
Complications are excuses.
Like tangled wire,
complications unravel to become one linear object.

Nils Glass received a call on his cell phone. It was his boss, who asked him if he would be coming into work anytime soon, that he hadn't shown up for several days, that it was bad enough it took Nils three months to decide on a typeface for his latest ad while collecting a full-time salary, but now he wasn't showing up to work. Nils responded by telling his boss that he would, in fact, not be returning to work, and to kindly fuck off.

After hanging up the phone he searched through his voicemail, which he had neglected for, apparently, several days, though it didn't feel like it at all. The hospital had called him a number times, as well as his in-laws. They were pressuring him to make a decision. The hospital was mostly certain that Sam would never regain consciousness, and her brain activity had been on a steady decline until now. There was hardly anything left, and her family wanted her to be taken off life support. Nils thought keeping her alive was the right choice—or at least, he had preferred that, because it bought him time to deflect the situation altogether. The voicemails started out as casual hellos, and updates from the hospital, but turned hostile from both the physicians and the in-laws after the third or fourth calls.

He wanted to curl up in a hole and die.

"Can we go back to the hospital. I need to decide," Nils asked the bone-man.

"You're not ready yet."

"You think I'll do the wrong thing?"

"It doesn't matter what you do. I think I know what you'll do, but right now, you're not going to do anything at all. Not with your wife anyway."

The bone-man wasn't really there then, but there was somebody sitting beside him on the stone bench. It was a teenage boy, a student perhaps, and he was reading a magazine. *Teenage boys don't read magazines. They might look at the pictures in magazines, but they certainly don't read magazines like* Forbes *on a park bench by themselves.* Nils suspected that if he turned to look at the boy's face that his eyes would not be in the text in his hand, but on something else, so he looked out. Sure enough, there was a girl there, all blonde and youthful just like in the movies. She wore glasses and had her nose buried into a book. Nils was too far away to tell what the book was. But he bet that the boy knew what it was.

"You know, son," Nils Glass said, "just because she likes to read doesn't mean *you* have to like to read."

The boy lowered the magazine.

"I mean, she probably doesn't care. I'd bet you've got something else in common that you won't have to lie about?" He turned and looked at the boy, he was staring at Nils, a little surprised that this strange adult was talking to him, but also thinking hard about what he had said.

Finally, the boy responded. "She goes to a book club. Or um, a reader's club. And they talk about books and articles and things. She's really smart. I'm not all that smart. But I figure I could go and start up a conversation there. Gotta read something."

"Not a bad plan," he responded. "That's how I met my wife. Well, sort of. She used to be on a bowling team. We played together once, her and I and some mutual friends."

"What happened?"

"She kicked my ass. I can't bowl to save my life. But we didn't talk much. Total failure. We didn't get together until a year later. A friend let it slip that she liked me, and it wasn't until then that I had the courage to talk to her. Point is, I lost a whole year."

"Man. You regret it?"

"Boy, you don't even know what regret is."

"You think I should talk to her now?"

"You could. Won't make a difference. All you're going to find out is what's still going to be the truth a year from now. I think."

Look at me, playing the wise old guy in the park.
There's a point to this...who's going to die?

"Hey kid."

"Yeah?"

"Go talk to her right now. Tell her exactly what you feel. If it's that you are in love with her, tell her that. If it's that you think her legs are nice and maybe you want to explore, tell her that. But *don't* tell her things you want her to hear, and don't tell her things that aren't the truth. Go on now, she's about to leave."

"How can you tell?"

"She's looking forward to see how many pages are left in the chapter. Means she's getting tired. Good opportunity. Here, give me this."

Nils snatched up the copy of *Forbes*.

"Ask her what she's reading. That's it. If you don't know what it is, don't pretend to. She'll probably enjoy telling you about it. Pay attention, but don't pretend to be interested if you aren't."

Then the boy got up. Nils Glass didn't stay to see what happened. Or rather, that's probably how it appeared to the boy, who looked for him after making a date with the girl. It was night now, and Nils was on the same bench, and the park was empty. He looked out at the place where the young man had been shot. He could see the same young man there, standing by himself, in his loose clothes and his beanie—the old man from the antique shop walked up to him, and patted him on the shoulder.

"Did they know each other?" Nils asked.

"Yes."

"Did you know them?"

"No," said the young waitress. She was wearing a black pencil skirt now, somewhat unsuitable for the cold, but not entirely out of place. More of an office look.

He watched as the old man turned about and walked away from the young man.

"Did they have to die?" he asked.

The waitress said nothing. Nils looked at her and found her neither desirable nor undesirable. She was a dead thing now. She was his desire—his unfulfilled desire, which he quenched, and then destroyed. He knew that. But what was the old man? He was just sick and elderly.

"He was the viewpoint," said the voice of the bone-man. "It wasn't as much about the man as it was the window."

"The boy with the drugs? I mean—I assumed..."

"They were. It's true. They meant something. Shame maybe."

"You don't know?" said the waitress to the bone-man.

"I am the guide to the destruction of destructive emotions. I am clarity."

"Clarity." Nils muttered to himself. Then his cell phone rang, and he answered it.

"Nils, you sonofabitch! Where in God's name have you been? Look, I don't care what the fuck it is that's keeping you, but Sam is dying and miserable and it's time to let go. So either get your ass down here now and pull the plug or go jump off a bridge and let us do it."

Click.

"Sam's uncle. He's at the hospital with her mother." He looked at the bone-man, who said nothing. "I'm going there, now. I'm done waiting."

Nils walked off.

"You're letting him go?" asked the waitress.

The old man walked over and said, "It was the first time he didn't ask a question about it, and just said what it was he planned to do."

"That's all it took?" she replied. "It was that simple?"

"Life and death are filled with complications, but in the end, they are made of simple things."

"Will he do the right thing?" asked the young man with the beanie.

The hooded figure touched his skeletal-muscular face. "I think he'll do the right thing, and he'll reap the rewards."

"But he doesn't know his wife will wake up tomorrow," said the waitress.

"If he loves her," said the teenage boy, "then he'll do the right thing."

"But does he love her?" asked the waitress.

The bone-man clicked his jaw. "You're all missing the point. It's not about her waking up. It's about him. And you," he regarded the teenage boy. "You shouldn't be here. If you're here, then we don't have much time."

V.

We are made of things.
Some of these things are necessary, others are not.
But we do miss these unnecessary things.
After all,
not needing something, does not prevent the pain.
The want amplifies the need that was not there to begin
with.

He stood outside of the hospital and watched his breath drift into the cold air. It was as if no time had passed at all. Sure, the ambulance pulling up *seemed* to be the same as the one that had pulled up some days ago, if maybe the driver was different. It made Nils Glass feel slightly less insane.

He walked in through the automatic sliding-glass doors, pushed passed a group of people waiting in front of the elevator to get to the stairs. Being in a confined space, controlled by an elevator's pace was repulsive to him. He was in control, moving up the stairs deliberately, skipping every other step up to the sixth floor without faltering.

Sam's mother was there, in the hospital room, but he locked eyes with her uncle first. He was a big man to be sure, fit though he was in his late fifties. The uncle raised a finger like he was about to give Nils a scolding the way a father scolds a child who hasn't come home on time, but Sam's mother stood up from the chair by the window and put a hand on her brother's shoulder. He pursed his lips, sighed, and put his palms and forehead against the wall in exasperation.

"Please, Nils. I can't do this anymore," said Sam's mother.

Nils took a few steps into the room and looked over at Sam, his wife, Linda. She was this artificially living thing on a slab of blankets, but she was his. He walked closer so that he could inspect every detail of her face. He knew this face like he knew the ridges in his own hands. He had looked at it night after night in the bed that they shared for years. He couldn't remember now how many it had been. Her lips were dry and cracked, and she had lost weight, every unnecessary ounce of mass.

So completely familiar, and yet I don't feel like I know you at all.

He replayed the past years. The other women he had been with, the fights, and the hatred that had tempered his love. He thought about his job, his interns, and how this had complicated everything further.

But life was really made of simple things. He had no job now. He had no wife, not really. In a way, he wanted to keep her alive just to spite her family. But was that really a good reason to prolong this? Everything would be so simple the moment she was gone. He would never again have to speak with her family, nor would he have to hide his marriage from strangers he met at parties and meetings.

He was confused, standing there looking at her and thinking about a world without her, though she was already gone. Nothing felt right. The other two people in the room were so quiet. Sam was there, but she was not. He felt the gun, which had remained perched in the waist of his pants.

"Are you there?" he said aloud, but the bone-man did not respond. "Are you there!?" he said again, this time louder and more nervously.

There was the voice of Sam's mother, muffled as if by a body of water, saying, "Nils, are you okay?"

What was it all for?

"Why didn't you tell me what it all was for?"

He pulled the gun from his waist and held it out to the side.

"Nils! What the hell do you think you're doing?"

He whipped around and pointed the gun at Sam's uncle, and he turned pale in a second.

"What's he doing?" asked the young man in the beanie.

"He's making a decision," said the old man, sipping his tea.

The waitress sighed. "This is the passion within him. He might not be stable enough to face the real world."

"Shut up! All of you!" Nils's eyes were mad and shaking in his head. Sam's mother looked terrified, and she was a strong woman, one Nils had respected and had lost arguments with time and again.

He raised the gun up to his own chin.

"Wait, stop!" shouted the bone-man with the hard ivory skin clad in shadows who now stood before him.

"Life *and* death are made of simple things," Nils muttered as he pulled the trigger.

He felt no pain and didn't really even hear the sound of the gun firing, though the lingering reverberation of the harmonics rang out in his head. He could still see the figure in front of him. It was bleeding a vivid crimson stream of blood from below the jawbone. Nils felt his own neck, and that it was dry.

The voices stopped, and the bone-man was gone, and the people were gone. He stood utterly alone in a silent space, feeling absolutely nothing. No fear, or remorse, or caring. Nothing. Nils turned to walk out.

It did not matter that the hospital room might have contained a hysterical and confused mother-in-law, or that it might have contained his wife just as she had been the day he stood out in the cold to visit some strange number of days ago, or even that it was possible that there was nobody in the hospital room at all. It did not matter. It did not matter that he was leaving a hospital, since he could have very well been leaving a park, or a diner, or a shop.

Nils Glass simply walked away, and that was that.

He didn't give a damn. If he could have felt anything at all, he probably would have felt content, he thought.

He thought.

VI.

Nils looked past his feet, over the edge of the concrete at the track over which the train would soon be passing. The teenage boy stood beside him and had been fidgeting awkwardly with his hands in his pockets for several minutes. Nils had counted the minutes. Time seemed to be moving at a pace he could keep track of now, though it gave him no comfort.

"People jump in sometimes," said the boy. "You know, they really do. It's pretty common. I didn't know people ever really *did* those sorts of things."

Nils said nothing. He wondered how a boy—one of a group of people who seemed by all accounts to be omniscient, at least in union—could not be aware of that. *Of course* people threw themselves in front of trains.

"You know," said the old man. "If I had asked *you* a moment ago, you would have thought the same thing."

"What's that?" Nils asked, and then bit his tongue in understanding. "Right. I guess you're right."

"I've seen more things, been more places. You have *that*," he let out breath, something like a laugh stifled before surfacing, "to look forward to."

The train came and went, a roaring cacophony of metal and wind, horn blaring through the industrial framework and echoing about the stones, then a fading memory of decaying reverberations.

"He's upset, you know," said the boy.

Nils stepped back from the track. "Someone's got to be."

"I'm serious!" His voice became insistent, whining, like a child pleading to get out of their chores. "You had a chance to change things and you missed it."

"Haven't things changed?"

He stomped his foot impatiently. "Not a bit! You ran away like a coward. You tried to take the easy way out. People *do try* to jump in front of trains. You're pathetic, Nils Glass."

"I thought I was doing the right thing."

The old man coughed and said, "But there's the rub. Listen here—the older you get the more you come to realize that there aren't any 'right things' at all."

"There was a *plan*," the boy said, exasperated.

"Sorry to disappoint," Nils said plainly. "Been doing that my whole life."

Then they were gone, and it was just the boneman and Nils, and they were once again in the park.

"Why do you keep bringing me here?" he asked the skeleton. "Heard you were upset at me."

"I didn't bring you here at all, Nils. You did. This is the last place you remember, isn't it?"

"I've never been to this place before. I'm sick of this, okay. I just want get out of here, to be done."

"*Think*, Nils, *think*." The being before him was becoming less skeletal, less human, and more shadow. "I'm done trying to fix you. You failed, and it's time to face the reality of your situation. Now, take a moment and tell me why you came here."

He looked around, for a way out, a way to run, but he knew running was pointless. The park—it was just a park. Nothing remarkable about it. Behind him, cars passed by on a busy street. Down that street was the antique shop. He had passed by the shop earlier; he knew that much. But why?

He was running. That's right. He felt a strange discomfort in his groin, in his back, and his brow was covered in sweat. He was not sweating though as a result of the running. The sweat had already been there.

His cell phone rang. He pulled it out, and it displayed a name in blue light. Sam was calling him. How could she be calling him? He would be at work, she knew that. She never called unless it was an emergency. Voicemail, listen to that.

Nils. Listen, Jeff just called me. He told me about Penny...

There was a pause filled with static, and it was long and uncomfortable.

I'm not mad...but we need to talk. Come home when you get this.

A knot twisted in his stomach. He flashed back to feeling of Penny's body on his just a half hour before. She was one of his interns. She brought him the wrong dry-cleaning, and when she moved around the corner into the storage supply closet, he entered, and they had sex. Jeff must have heard them.

Nils couldn't blame Jeff for calling Sam, but he desperately wanted to smack him in the face about now. Suddenly the ecstasy he had felt was tarnished and only fed into the panic he was suffering. This probably wouldn't end his relationship, but he did not want to have the conversation he was about to have. Jeff couldn't have been aware that the affair had been going on for months, starting with the Cola ad shoot. The diner set was where he'd met penny, where he felt alive for the first time in years.

He walked to his car, wearing the suede coat that was not his, the wrong dry cleaning, sat in silence for a few moments before starting the engine and driving home. On his way, he purchased something at a small shop that a co-worker had told him about some days prior. He bought a little glass figurine, with the hopes of offering it to Sam when he got home, not that it would make anything better. He had done that often, tried to deflect the reality with alluring trinkets. It never worked, but she could never say he didn't try. The little man in the shop who sold the figurine to him had asked if it was for a special person.

"No," Nils responded, "it's not." And the old man gave a look that made Nils want to shoot the man. He looked confused, judgmental, and this displeased him. It wasn't really the shopkeeper's fault, but it was easy to project his own problems onto complete strangers than have to deal with them himself.

"Very good, Nils," said the old man, and his voice was echoed by the bone-man.

"But who am I?" said the young man with the beanie.

Nils shook his head. He didn't know.

The teenaged boy wrung his *Forbes* magazine. "What happened when you got home?"

"I don't know!" Nils replied, exasperated.

"Did you stay there?" asked the young man.

He was walking back down the stairs of the building, away from their comfortable apartment. Sam was with him.

"She asked to go for a walk…"

And then they were in the park. He didn't remember the conversation, but that it made him less uncomfortable than he had expected. She was calm and even hooked her arm around his when they walked out into the cold. They talked for a long time, or at least she did, and Nils would hum affirmative responses to show that he was listening.

"You're not half bad at relationship advice," said the teenaged boy.

Nils shivered in the cold. His body was in pain, but he was only aware of it. He did not feel it.

"All I did was tell you what I *should* have done when I was you."

The bone-man's blurred smoky form descended over him, and the voice became less human and more memorable. For the first time, he heard its words clearly.

"A visit from your younger self is an omen of the end. We don't have much time. Now, *think*."

He saw the young man out in the park. The sound of the bullet rang out and he fell to the floor. The others with the guns looked over at Nils and Sam. She clutched his shoulder, and another shot was fired. Her legs fell out from beneath her and she nearly pulled him down.

Without letting go, Nils got down and placed her on the sidewalk. There were vaguely reverberant sounds of his own voice calling her name in the night. It didn't matter that the men with the guns were walking towards him. There was only her. She was breathing, and he didn't know why. The bullet had pierced her skull, yet she was somehow alive.

He thought only of the future, the uncomfortable knot in his stomach writhing within him. She would go to the hospital, and Nils would have to care for her. She would never be the same, and he would have to quit his job, never hear her voice again, and his life would become a mess of family phone calls, painful decisions, and complications. He imagined himself walking up into a hospital room having to decide whether to pull the plug on her or not. It was absurd; she was dying and would never get to a hospital on time. But there were sirens already wailing throughout the streets.

"And then what happened?" The bone-man was no longer a figure, but a cloud of black redness cascading in layers across his vision, blinding him with reality. Another shot rang out.

And then, Nils Glass realized what had happened. He stood in darkness and tried to feel his body, his true body. It was warm, and the same as it had all these timeless days, and there was a pressure on his back, as though he were laying on it. He could hear chatter and the rustling of curtains on metal rings dragging along metal rods, the beeping and whirring of machines and the pinch of a needle in his arm. The sensation of his bladder draining.

"Am I going to die?"

The voice of the bone-man that he knew was present there did not answer right away. When it did, Nils thought he sensed sadness, or maybe regret.

"I expect so."

Nils shuttered, though he was unsurprised, and asked why the bone-man had gone through the trouble of bringing his situation to light for him, to which the disembodied voice said plainly, "It's because you are in recovery mode, and now you can wake up, if you like."

"You said I was going to die."

"That is why you get the choice. If you were going to live, you would be awake already."

"You all could have just asked me up front. It would have been easier than going through the whole song and dance."

"It's no trouble, your brain did all the work. Besides, if you were sitting with your wife in a hospital room within a false reality you would be in no position to make such a decision."

Nils did not think the decision was hard at all. Either way he was going to die. This issue was whether or not he would be able to say goodbye to anyone. It was a matter of facing his own death or going peacefully in his sleep. He didn't really have anybody to say good-bye to anyway. Sam was probably in the bed beside him. There was nothing he had to say to her, and nothing she would hear. Her family would be there, not his. It was never about keeping Sam alive or pulling the plug, it was about letting himself wake up and face the complicated world outside. *But really*, he thought, *it was all so simple*.

"I think I'd rather not."

"Sam will wake up tomorrow too, if she chooses."

Nils shrugged. "We talked, before we were shot. Nothing was going to be the same. If we both wake up, I'll die later and have to finish the conversation before I go. If she wakes up and I don't, things will be easier for her. I'll already be gone, and she'll move on." The sensation in his false limbs were fading away, and so was the presence around him. "I'm done. But thanks for trying…"

Bones clicked from a distance, "Thanks for the French toast. Good luck, Nils."

"Hey, wait. I have a question."

"Yes, Nils?"

"If this was all happening in my head, how do you all—*we* all know so many things?"

There was silence for a moment.

"That's all bit complicated, something to do with the subconscious taking hold as you near the release of consciousness to the universe."

"I see," said Nils.

The Afterimage of Patrick Samson

I

A man sat on a bench outside the coffee shop on the corner, sipping something steaming, intently watching the opposite corner of the road and severely overcompensating in his effort to appear casual. Cars buzzed by, noticing nothing in the world let alone this fairly regular fellow wearing a regular faded blue-black suit, a regular black leather briefcase at his feet. The street was busy, but quiet in the way that the beach feels quiet even though hundreds of tons of water are crashing over fine rocks at regular intervals. Regularity drained all sense of chaos and entropy, from the man, from the city, from the world.

It was a Thursday, so the shops were not expecting business, and the man enjoyed the peace, that special sort of city peace that only someone originally from a city would consider peace, with the cars whipping gusts of air into the soundscape and the people going in and out of shops—but at least the cars were not honking horns or slamming doors and the people were not running to get to their next destination—and a comfortable temperature. Peace. And that was something the man enjoyed about Thursdays.

His eyes were fixed across the street, only occasionally would he flick his eyes toward another corner or someone passing by him on the sidewalk, but always returned to the corner opposite him.

The man took a sip and looked at the silver watch on his left wrist, polished, clean, and 8:57am. He inhaled the steam coming from his cup and let out a relaxed sigh, the sort of breath one takes before picking up the phone for a call they know will bring bad news. He set his cup on the ground beside the bench next to a couple discarded cigarettes that were not his, keeping his eyes glued to the same point in space across the street.

8:59, and he began to get nervous.

9:01, and he began to clench his teeth.

9:05, and he was practically sweating with anxiety.

9:07, he saw it.

He bolted up from the bench, grabbing his briefcase and eyeing that thing for which he waited and watched. Another had walked around the corner, slightly later than expected *irregular*, a tall gentleman in a grey suit this particular morning and a matching hat. His hair was black, excepting a few visible grey patches over his ears, and pulled back into a tight ponytail swinging a foot and a half beneath the brim of his hat with each step. He walked diligently down the sidewalk, in a hurry, but not rushed, and not taking a moment to look around at any other people or place.

Our man with the briefcase followed him from across the street, his head cocked to the left, eyes focusing on the person for which he had been waiting. At the end of the block he would cross the street to meet the other man's path and pursue him more directly.

This other man with the ponytail and grey suit began to walk more briskly, bounding steps eventually becoming a jog and finally a light run to which our man across the street matching with every step in his pursuit, pushing past a few window-shoppers peering into expensive boutiques. He had little trouble keeping up but did have to loosen his tie a bit and wipe his brow with a free hand. The corner was coming up.

Our man gripped his briefcase tightly by the handle and made a sharp pivot to the left, running into the crosswalk with all haste, his head turning to keep focused on the other man who continued straight on his path. He would be able to keep up easily, even with the lost time; he knew he was the faster. He *knew* this other man's pace.

The city peace was broken as a car blew its horn, breaking our man's unyielding focus at last just before slamming into his body. Our man gripped his briefcase with both arms to his chest and rolled over the hood of the car, pushing one arm underneath himself to propel off the back, landing squarely on his feet behind the vehicle.

The driver hurriedly opened the door and emerged, a young woman in her mid-twenties in business casual, hair pulled back and up, and very frantic.

"Oh my god! Are you okay?"

The man rubbed his eyes and the bridge of his nose, and said, without looking at her, "Yes, I'm fine."

"Fine? I just hit you with my car!" she started to pace, "I'm so sorry, I should've been watching, but you ran right out, I didn't have time to stop. Oh my God, please don't call the police, I can't–"

"Is it damaged?" the man said, eager to get out of the situation as quickly as possible.

"What?" she said, puzzled.

"Your car, is it damaged?" He kept his focus out in the same direction as his original path.

"The car? I–," at a glance she could see a dent had indeed been made on the hood upon impact, but she paid little notice to it as she circled the vehicle and returned to him, tripping awkwardly over her heels, "it's fine, no big deal, are you sure you're okay?"

"Here," the man said, pulling a black business card from his breast pocket. He handed it to her and looked back to see that he had lost sight of the man he was pursuing, "*shit.*"

Our man ran off in the direction of the other, ignoring the nervous protests of the woman standing outside her car flagging him down in the middle of the road.

The woman sighed as she lost sight of him. Drivers were honking their horns as they moved around her and her vehicle. She looked down at the black card she received and read the gold script:

M. Caldwell, CPA
07700-900645

--

The man Caldwell rushed down an alley, a shortcut between two buildings that would presumably make up for the time lost from his accident, that is, if the man with the ponytail followed his regular route, and

Caldwell hoped dearly that he would. First, because there would be no chance of locating the man if he had made a detour; second, because a detour meant that the man might be performing irregular actions without his knowing.

He made a right turn and found himself facing his person of interest.

The man was looking directly at Caldwell, speaking, but no sound came from his mouth, and when Caldwell began to move the man made no alteration to his focus but continued to speak and gesture, muted.

"Who are you talking to, Samson?" Caldwell said, more to himself than to the silent ponytailed man.

He looked up at the building to his right, a collection of offices. The door listed a few names of doctors, an orthopedic surgeon, a dentist, two family practitioners, and a single name that was recognized—a coroner. He looked back at Samson, who had stopped his silent conversation at an unknown target, adjusted his hat, and pulled a sum of cash from his pocket, handing it out in front of him. He released his grip and the sum vanished. Samson nodded, stood for a moment, and began walking at a relaxed pace—stepping forward and passing directly through Caldwell.

It had no effect on our man Caldwell, who stood staring at the name on the door, the coroner, James Kim. He memorized the name and turned to follow the other man called Samson once more, at a closer distance, observing, as he did every day, that this man was faintly transparent, like a faded recording. While at last loosening his grip on the briefcase, he followed this faded man as he had for days, the world around recalibrating regularity.

II

Ana Leigh walked into her apartment, kicking off her heels, letting down her hair with a routine flourish, and tossing her coat over the back of the leather sofa she rarely used. By habit, she made her way to the kitchen and poured herself a small glass of sparkling wine. The bottle was half empty, one of many bottles she received as gifts from work, from bosses, donors, or men trying to impress her. There were so many that she disregarded her original idea that they should be saved for special occasions. "Special" in this case, meaning any occasion in which she would not be spending her evening alone in her apartment. She would be drowning in bowed and wrapped bottles of wine had she kept to this rule and constantly reminded about countless birthdays and holidays spent by herself, not entirely, but at least partially, out of choice.

So she drank them, slowly, never more than one glass after work. She sat on a stool at the bar of her counter and looked around at the familiar setting. It was a nice apartment, expensive, but cozy; and decorated professionally with contemporary decor to which she had never given much thought. A hall and doorway led to her bedroom, and the wall adjacent to the kitchen was tinted glass with a beautiful view of the city lights.

She stared at the phone sitting on the counter beside her. As ordinary as this evening was for her it had been a very unordinary sort of day. This was mainly because earlier that morning she had hit a man with her car on her way to work.

Tonight, she would be pouring that second glass.

The man had run out into the road, quite abruptly, without making any effort to observe the traffic around him. Ana, of course, hadn't really been paying very close attention herself, or she might've seen the other cars braking and swerving to avoid him. But the collision was inevitable, as two clearly unfocused individuals crossed paths. The man in the faded blue suit had seemed rather focused, too focused to heed the traffic and quite in a hurry to get on his way. He certainly didn't seem to be hurt even though Ana had been traveling about forty-five miles per hour when she struck him.

She continued eyeing the black card the man had given her, particularly the name, *M. Caldwell*, in gold script. It seemed so very old-fashioned, the name, the type, everything about the card was dated. She wondered if she should call the number below. Obviously, he had indented her to call him to discuss the damage to her car, or to himself. Why else would he giver her his card? Of course, she wondered why he would be concerned with damage to her car at all. It was the first time she'd ever hit a pedestrian, so she wasn't sure exactly what to expect, but she certainly didn't think the pedestrian owed anything to the driver.

Ana set down her glass, now half empty, picked up the receiver and dialed.

A ring.

"Caldwell," said the man's voice. She was surprised the answer came on the first ring.

"Hi, this is Ana Leigh, Mr. Caldwell. I hit you with my car earlier today."

"Yes, I believe it was an Audi."

Ana heard what sounded like a door shutting from the other end of the line and, looking up at the wall clock, noticed how late it was.

"Yes," she responded, "um..."

"I suppose you have some kind of estimate of the damage to your vehicle?"

"Oh, no... I haven't," she hadn't thought to do that. She had been out of sorts after the initial hit. "Yes, I suppose that's why you gave me your card..."

"Yes, that would be why," he said, little inflection in his voice.

Ana found no comfort in his tone or response, but she did have an aversion to think poorly of him, possibly because she supposed he was a slightly attractive, mostly because there wasn't anything malicious about his behavior. She twisted her hair around a finger and bit her lip in a way she hadn't done since she was in school, and promptly slammed her hand against her counter in defiance of herself.

"Miss?"

"I'm sorry... so I suppose I'll call you back then."

A light sigh over the phone, "Yes, just tell me where to send the check."

"Right, I'm at 925 3rd, apartment 10b."

"Great, let me know then. And, try not to walk around alone."

Click.

She put the phone back down, more confused than ever. What did he mean to do by warning her not to walk around alone? It certainly didn't seem like any sort of threat. He seemed to be genuinely concerned, in a pragmatic sort of way, the way a doctor warns a patient to get lots of rest and to drink fluids when they're ill.

Elsewhere, yet another man, in neither a faded blue nor a grey suit, walked with brisk and firm intent. This man wore a black quarter-length jacket of high quality, hand-made from another time and place, and had short wavy hair, a choreographed mess of black with sporadic premature grays catching bits of light from the street lamps. His fingers fidgeted nervously at his sides, his eyes shooting from one point to another keeping careful track of every night pedestrian, every lit window, and the occasional whir of a passing car. Of all the men mentioned thus far, wearing some sort of suit, walking with brisk intent, this man, who is called Mr. 3, was the most neurotic, the most irregular.

When Mr. 3 arrived, he did not knock at the frosted glass window of the dark green door, or ring, or call to enter. He did not use a key or enter a code. He simply placed his hand on the handle and entered, knowingly invited, did not wipe his shoes, having made his way up a flight of stairs, down an unlit hallway covered in debris. He stood in the doorway for a moment before fully entering and saw two men. The first and most important was sitting behind a desk. Mr. 3 drew from beneath his jacket a photograph of one Ana Leigh.

"He made contact today," the man called 3 said, "spoke for about one and a half minutes to this woman."

"A record for our Caldwell," the man behind the desk said, "circumstances?"

"I believe she hit him with her car while he was pursuing an afterimage."

The man behind the desk was older, with a white and grey beard, who's suit color often changed, and with a massive build. This man was Mr. 1.

"Well it seems he's using his skills again," said Mr. 1, cracking his knuckles, "unlike this one."

Mr. 3 then acknowledged the second man that had already been in the office and who lay face-down on the floor with a knife in his back.

"Ah, right."

III

"Ana, I need deliverables by 3:00. I'm being generous."

"Yes sir, Mr. Edwards," Ana replied shortly.

"Don't give me a tone, Leigh, I don't need that right now. You know that."

She said nothing as Edwards walked away. The man was a creep and had spent half of his time making her job miserable and the other half trying to get Ana to fuck him. At least eight of the fifteen bottles of wine in her apartment had come from Edwards at one point or another. The fact that he could switch between trying to be charming and casually acting like an ass-hole made Ana think he assumed they were already a couple.

Ana worked at a bank, the corporate offices of a global entity that had recently been acquired by the Glover Group. Several changes had already started to occur, including Edwards being made her supervisor, which hadn't made a bit of sense since he was an accountant and she was in marketing.

The Glover Group's acquisition of the bank was one of many companies that was part of a sweeping takeover. Though the group was known for incredibly fair pay (Ana had received a substantial raise along with much of the staff) and a generally scandal-free administration, she had an uneasy feeling about the whole business of it.

Edwards circled back to Ana's desk less than ten minutes later.

"I'm leaving for a conference and won't be back for the rest of the day. We're going out for drinks afterwards. If you're done with all of your work by 6:00 tonight you ought to join us."

Ana couldn't tell if he cared more about her completing her work or about joining him for drinks. Honestly, it was as though he was trying to be as ambiguous as possible, perhaps so that he wouldn't be accused of harassment.

"Yes, we'll see Mr. Edwards."

There was no way in hell.

After work, Ana walked home, taking the long way. She had postponed getting her car looked at despite the minimal cosmetic damage. It wouldn't be a problem to repair and only a minor inconvenience to be without a car for a day or two. She enjoyed the walk. At first, she had planned to walk to work and test out the route before she took her car in, and over the next few days it became a habit. The city sounded very different from the inside of a car, the strange sounds made stranger through the filter of glass windows. She had expected it to be loud, the cars racing by, the pedestrians talking on their cell phones, but it had been surprisingly peaceful, unlike the noise of her car and the wind rushing by at high speeds.

There was another reason she had postponed the service. It would mean that she would have to get back in touch with the man Caldwell.

She wasn't nervous about the phone call itself. Ana made numerous calls every day at work to people far more difficult, and Caldwell seemed well-mannered and imperturbable, a pleasant relief from the men who either patronized her or overtly attempted to show their chivalry in hopes that she would be impressed and therefore forthcoming with her body. No, it wasn't the act of contacting him; it was that she had a reluctance to bring closure to their unresolved business. Once all was said and done she would have no reason to contact the man at all, and that would be that.

She considered the fact that she was making no contact with him presently, but the prospect, the idea that there was some pending agreement, some link to him, was exciting to her. Again, she considered her mild attraction to him. She was allowed that after all. Men gawked at her, made degrading comments, but she could empathize to some degree despite her reeling and repeated frustration. She objectified the men around her too, acknowledging though that she was far more discreet about it.

What she had not thought about much was the man's strange comment about not walking alone, and she hadn't been reminded of it until she was confronted with two suited bodies that could have been men or women. Each had a hood that came out from under their suit coats and covered their heads and shrouded their faces. The sun had since set and the light of the passing cars and streetlights only served to highlight the short knives that each figure carried.

Ana stopped in her tracks and stood there silently for several moments. She thought it unlikely that she would be attacked on the sidewalk of a busy street. A passing car would surely see. But would they stop to help? She recalled hearing screams one night in a parking garage and told herself that it was probably some over excited teen or a startled pedestrian, putting out of her mind the idea that anyone would be getting assaulted in a public space, and certainly extinguishing any sense of responsibility for her to act or call the police.

Staring at the dark faces of the two suited people and their knives she found herself thinking only about the nameless individuals racing by in their cars and wondering if they would stop to help her. More importantly, she wondered if the potential assailants would be thinking the same thing, and if they cared at all.

There was a hand that touched her, gently, and just below her right shoulder blade.

She hadn't considered that there would be three of them, but it made sense. Two to distract her, and a third to grab her from behind. But the touch was not threatening. It served only to tell her that someone was now beside her. She could see the heads of the suited figures shift to look at whomever had come up behind her. They retracted their blades into the cuffs of their sleeves and backed away slowly, retreating into the shadows of a nearby alley.

Ana looked up at the person beside her, relieved to see the familiar face of the man she had hit with her car just a few days prior.

"Mr. Caldwell," she said.

He raised a finger to his lips, never looking at her. "Don't speak, Ms. Leigh. Run."

Before she could respond, he took hold of her wrist and began to run, leading her up the street. She looked back to see a number of figures where she had been standing just a moment before. Seven or eight of them, standing there, motionless, brandishing knives.

"What the fuck is this?" she said as stumbling became jogging. When she and Caldwell were at the same pace he released her wrist and led her through alleys Ana didn't know existed, between buildings that didn't make sense, though she could hardly visualize the scope of the city while fleeing for her life.

She didn't say "what the fuck" again until they were well inside the dark underside of an abandoned dock structure, and she said it repeatedly.

"What the fuck was that!?"

"Ms. Leigh."

"No! You tell me not to walk around alone with no context whatsoever and then this happens. Who are those people? I know you know!"

"Calm down."

"I will not calm—"

"*Calm down.*"

She was silent then. The tone of his voice had changed drastically.

"Ms. Leigh, I need to ask you some questions. Would that be acceptable?"

At first, she thought that he was simply trying to calm her down, but when she said nothing she realized that he was actually waiting for a response.

"If you tell me who those men were, and what's going on, then sure. I guess I'll talk to you. But first I want to know if we're safe here."

"We are safe here, Ms. Leigh."

She looked around at the decaying ruins of iron-works and could hear the sound of water moving under the docks. There were several entrances to the dock structure, half-collapsed walls where distant lights of the city slipped through, casting harsh shadows of the wood and steel and rubbish against the sides of what little structure had remained erect. It didn't seem safe at all. Despite what had just happened, she felt safer out on the streets of the city where she knew there were more than a single set of eyes on her.

Caldwell sensed her skepticism.

"*I* am safe here. I am safe everywhere from them. You are safe because you're under my protection now."

As much as she did not want to, she felt relieved by his words, reassured more by his voice and the presence than by the cold empty structure to which they had fled. She had few reasons to trust him, but fewer still to mistrust him, and what choice did she really have?

"What do you want to know, Mr. Caldwell?"

"I need to know something very personal, and I hope you'll forgive me for prying into a subject so sensitive. But I assure you that it is necessary."

Her face may have flushed. What did he want to ask her? Ana was grateful that they were in the darkness.

"Go ahead, Mr. Caldwell. I'll tell you what you need to know."

Caldwell spoke then, and despite the strange sequence of interactions with him, starting with a pedestrian accident in which he was unharmed and had offered his card to her, to his odd tone and warning on the phone, and even the attack by knife brandishing hooded figures, *this* was the moment that would stick with her as the strangest moment with our man Caldwell.

"Ms. Leigh, I need to know if your accounts are in order."

IV

Mr. 3 entered the office of Mr. 1, whose entire body was shrouded in the smoke of cigars, one which he held in his hand, and two others which sat, lit and untouched, on his desk.

Mr. 3 looked around to see that the body which had been on the floor the previous day had been removed by some method about which he could only speculate. Mr. 1 had a particular way of disposing of unwanted things, but Mr. 3 had not seen his superior perform such acts for many years. He decided not to bring it up, and silently placed a file on the desk.

"I found this in her apartment, sir."

"But you did not find her?"

Mr. 3 let out a weak laugh, something between a stutter and a whine. "We had hoped to ambush her, but she walked home, and when she did not arrive at her usual time we assumed Ms. Leigh made a detour of some sort and I sent my seconds after her."

Mr. 1 used the lit end of his cigar to flip the file open, igniting the corner of the manila card-stock and leaving a trail of ash on the desk. The singed corner burned across the collection of papers containing an assortment of Ana Leigh's mail. Mr. 1 glanced at each item and placed them back down one page at a time, each catching fire in sequence. Finally, he lifted the black business card and placed it aside on the desk.

"It seems our man has taken Ms. Leigh as a client."

Mr. 3 let out another strange laugh. "It would explain why we cannot access any of her accounts. She's under his protection now. So, what would you like me to do, sir?"

Mr. 1 moved his cigar to his left hand and picked up one of the untouched burning cigars from his desk.

"Do you remember when we smoked together, Mr. 3?"

"I never did sir."

"Not you," he said. "The three of *us*. We worked so well together. My poor heart misses those days. I still light a cigar for each of us. Perhaps one day we'll be whole again, able to go back to that time before everything fell apart."

Mr. 3 watched as Mr. 1 gazed longingly at the cigar in his massive hand, like a jeweler examining a fine and rare stone, watched as his superior directed the cigar down and pressed the burning end into the black business card.

"But that day will never come, 3, because one of our men is dead, and our man Caldwell is as good as dead to me now. I haven't been this upset in decades," Mr. 1 said calmly, with no inflection in his voice whatsoever.

"No..." he said picking up the card and staring at Mr. 3 through the hole now burned through the center. "That's not right. *Hungry*. I have not been this hungry in decades."

Mr. 3 let out another nervous laugh and tried not to think of where the body on the office floor had gone.

V

Our man Caldwell stood impatiently in Ana Leigh's living room.

"Ms. Leigh, I'm afraid my associate will not wait for me if I'm late. It's very important that we are on time."

Ana's voice came from her bedroom around the corner. "If I'm going to be held hostage by you then I am at least going to get a change of clothes and more comfortable shoes."

"I'll remind you that you are *not* my hostage. You are my client, and I can't keep you safe if you go out on your own."

She emerged, wearing a blue zip-up hoodie, black leggings, and a pair of brightly colored sneakers. "What?"

"It's nothing, are you ready?"

Ana nodded. "If I can't go to work then there's no reason in dressing like it. Hope that's okay with you."

Caldwell shook his head and led Ana Leigh out of the apartment and into the elevator down the hall.

"So," she began, "if I'm your client, does that mean I can fire you whenever I want?"

"It would be foolish, and I would require it in writing, but technically, yes you could."

"Have you been fired before?"

Caldwell inhaled deeply. "Not once. In fact, my portfolio of clients includes some who are long deceased. People who begin a professional relationship with me find it in their best interest not to end it, ever."

"So, does this mean you're going to follow me until I die?"

"Of course not," Caldwell responded, "when it is clear that those who are coming after you have ceased we will continue a more appropriate level of correspondence."

"And what will you be to me then?" she asked.

"I will be your accountant, that is all, Ms. Leigh."

They moved through the lobby and walked out onto the busy sidewalk. A black car was parked there, a suited driver holding the rear door open.

"This is us," Caldwell said.

The driver smiled and tipped his hat to Ana. "Good morning, Ms. Leigh. Mr. Caldwell."

"Good morning," Ana replied as she slipped into the car.

She had only been in a car like this a few times before, when she worked as an intern on the failed re-election campaign of the governor. She stopped working in politics after that. Despite the results of the election, she had done a good job and impressed her supervisor, who had been deputy campaign manager and was also a partner at the agency at which Ana was now currently employed. She made more money now but was hit with the nostalgia of riding in the backs of large black cars among motorcades, the leather seats and small tabletops being the closest thing to an office she ever had.

Just a few blocks down the road, Ana noticed they were pulling up to a sidewalk where a man in a grey suit was waiting. She recognized this as the same street that she had accidentally hit Caldwell with her car.

The driver put the car in park, exited and walked around the vehicle to open the door for the man in the grey suit, who took the passenger seat.

Ana couldn't see the man's face, only that his hair was long and pulled into a tight ponytail. He wore a hat that matched his grey suit.

"Good morning," Ana said.

The man in the passenger seat did not respond. Perhaps it was the light coming through the window, but there seemed to be an odd quality about him, something Ana could not quite identify.

"That man," Caldwell said, "is Patrick Samson. The former head of a notable organization that built many of the buildings in the city."

The man Samson was silent and unmoving. The driver did not show any signs that he was returning into the car. He simply waited on the sidewalk.

"Mr. Caldwell," Ana said nervously. "What's going on?"

"Look," Caldwell said quietly. "He's starting to sweat."

Sure enough, the hair around Samson's ears was beginning to shine, and a drip of cold sweat ran down his neck."

"It isn't the summer," Caldwell continued, "because he's wearing his winter suit and hat. He isn't speaking, or moving, so he must be listening. He sits in the front seat, so it isn't his car. It's somebody else's, somebody in the backseat, speaking to him."

Ana looked back and forth from Samson to Caldwell. Caldwell had stopped explaining to Ana and was instead working through something in his own head aloud. His eyes were fixed on the man in the front seat.

"He sits in the front seat for five minutes before he gets out. So... who is he meeting?"

Samson's hand jerks and takes hold of the door handle, but he stops before pulling it. He turns his head to the backseat and looks at Ana.

"Don't worry," Caldwell said calmly. "It isn't you he's looking at. You weren't here, after all."

Samson's eyes began to widen, his lips parting, not to speak but as a result of the expression of a person who has just received very upsetting news. His breathing became heavier.

Ana looked directly in the man's eyes, seeing fear, but feeling that the man was not seeing her at all. Then she suddenly understood what had been so strange about the man. It was not the light coming through the car, but the light coming through the man. He was opaque, his skin and his suit and his hat and his hair were all varying levels of transparent.

Samson's face became something sad and defeated then. He looked up at Ana one last time and mouthed silently, "I understand," then the door opened.

The driver had opened the passenger door again and there was a moment when Samson still made the motion as if he himself were pulling the handle and letting himself out.

She watched as Samson walked a few steps away, eyes moving as though he were watching a car drive away, but there were none on the road. He pulled his phone from his coat, dialed, and put it to his ear.

"That man," Caldwell said, "is dead. What you just saw was his afterimage, a sort of delayed replay of his life and actions. I've been watching him for some time, trying to piece together the little information I have on him."

The driver returned to his seat behind the wheel.

"Mr. Caldwell, would you like to stay and watch his conversation?"

"That won't be necessary," Caldwell responded to the driver. "I know what he's saying. This is the call he makes to his accountant, instructing him to relinquish his assets. The next call he makes will be to his CFO, instructing him to authorize the merger of his company with the Glover Group."

"Wait," Ana said, trying to wrap her head around what was going on. "*The* Glover Group? I know you said a prominent builder, but you mean that man's company was Skyland Properties?"

"Correct. And the third call he is about to make is to his wife, saying that he loves her, and that he's sorry."

"That merger happened over a year ago," Ana said slowly. "I remember reading that it happened after the CEO was found dead in the bay."

"That's certainly how it looked," Caldwell explained, "but it seems that his death was the result of the merger, and not the other way around. Ms. Leigh, you looked into his eyes. Tell me, what did you see? If you had to guess, what was he told in the car?"

She tried to come to terms with the idea that this phantom had just been paraded in front of her, and that Caldwell had presented it as simple fact. Ana looked at our man, seeing that he was seriously expecting an answer from her, and waiting patiently for it. She closed her eyes and replayed the short scene in her head.

"I'd say he was being threatened," she said at last.

"I think you would be correct, Ms. Leigh."

VI

"I've already told you twice, sir, I don't share personal information about any patient."

"You call them patients, Dr. Kim?"

Dr. James Kim removed his lab coat and hung it on the hook beside his office door. "Yes, I do. Just because I am a coroner does not mean that I treat confidential patient information any different. You'll need a subpoena if you want more Mr. ... What was your name again?"

The person with the cropped blonde hair smiled. "You may call me Mr. 4," said Mr. 4. "And I trust you'll be more forthcoming when you learn that your clinic is due to be repossessed at the end of the month."

"That's ridiculous, about as ridiculous as your ridiculous name! Get out, I didn't agree to this meeting to be threatened."

"No, Dr. Kim, but you did agree to it. And people who agree with me once tend to agree with me always. So, let's *sit and chat some more*." His tone was deliberate and slow, almost another language though the words were English.

Dr. Kim sat in his chair.

"Your lease on this building is now under the supervision of the Ledger Organization, and the rent is about to double. I know for a fact that half of your assets are still tied up in South Korea and your recent attempts to facilitate a partial transfer have gone undetected and untaxed. With rent about to go up, it would be in your best interest if they remained that way."

"Are you with the IRS?" Dr. Kim asked timidly, cold sweat beginning to collect around his temples.

"Oh no, Dr. Kim. I with a group far older and far more intrinsic to the movement of currency in this country. You're fortunate that I discovered your activity, and that the IRS is less resourceful than we. *Don't you feel fortunate.*" Again, his words became slow and rhythmic.

"Yes, Mr. 4. I feel very fortunate."

Mr. 4 smiled wide.

"Then give me what I want."

Dr. Kim nodded and stood. He walked over a filing cabinet and sifted through papers before removing a manila file and handing it over.

Mr. 4 smiled so wide his eyes shut. "The Ledger Group thanks you for your cooperation."

Mr. 4 exited the office and closed the door behind him. Mr. 3 was waiting there with his arms crossed.

"Did you get it?"

Mr. 4 handed the file over to Mr. 3. "Like candy from a baby. The money laundering was helpful but unnecessary. The man had no willpower whatsoever. Broke right away."

"Well, this is interesting…"

"What is it?"

Mr. 3 perused the file. "It appears that some evidence remained. If Caldwell had gotten ahold of this, it would have proven that the body found in the bay was not Samson's."

"So, what?" said Mr. 4. "Caldwell already knows that. We all know what happened to Samson's body."

"Yes but, this *proves* it. It's the sort of thing that gets people talking, and we're in a precarious state as it is."

"Ah, so what you're saying," Mr. 4 said turning to look at his colleague, "is that our superior would be upset to hear that you made such a careless mistake in covering our tracks."

Mr. 3 let out a nervous sighing laugh.

"Perhaps you should *tell him what you've found.*" Mr. 4 said slowly.

"Now stop that!" Mr. 3 snapped. "Don't try your tricks on me."

Mr. 4 let out a laugh and smiled wide.

"It's not funny, 4," said Mr. 3. "Our superior, he's…"

Mr. 4's smile faded. "What?"

"He's started again."

"Really?"

"Yes, he told me that he's been feeling hungry."

Mr. 4 stroked his chin. "Well I suppose we need to find something to feed him besides mistakes."

Mr. 3 nodded in agreement and they exited the coroner's clinic.

"Wait," Mr. 4 said. "So, does that mean Mr. 5…"

Mr. 3 nodded.

VII

"If you're going to haul me all over the city, you might as well tell me what's going on."

"Trust me, Ms. Leigh, my ability to keep you safe is contingent on the success of the audit of Patrick Samson's affairs."

Ana Leigh stopped in her tracks. "We'll I'm not moving until you tell me exactly who you are and who's coming after me. And you're *not* going to force me."

"Ms. Leigh, I hear your concerns loud and clear, but now really isn't the time."

She stood silent with her arms crossed.

He searched for a simple explanation. "I'm just an accountant, a dedicated one, Ms. Leigh."

She scoffed, unimpressed and unsatisfied. "Normal accountants don't barrel roll over speeding cars and investigate dead men."

"Accounting," he said, the word enunciated as though it were antiquated and sacred, "when you're as dedicated to the service as I am, can be a very dangerous job."

She laughed and rolled her eyes.

"What's funny about that?" asked Caldwell.

"You should meet the accountants at my job. They posture like corporate nobility in the office, but they shrivel when they get a paper cut."

Caldwell searched for meaning in her comment and continued to struggle in devising an explanation. "Every profession, I suppose, can be broken down into the amateur, professional, elite, or special force. The shopping center security guard is in the same field as the Secret Service, just a few levels down."

"I get it. So, you're kind of like a Navy SEAL of accounting, huh?"

"We all were," Caldwell said sadly.

At this, Ana uncrossed her arms. Realizing that he had misspoke and that the sun was beginning to set, he conceded.

"I'll tell you what you want to know if we can keep moving."

Ana agreed, and they continued to walk down the sidewalk, towards a tunnel at the edge of the city that she had never driven through before. The driver had taken them out of the city proper, and now the terrain was unfamiliar. The sidewalks grew more cracked and displaced the further the pair traveled, and graffiti was more prevalent until it was altogether absent.

They were walking toward what had once been a thriving convention center, one that Ana's father had brought her to when she had turned nine. He had offered to take her to the circus, but she said that she was more interested to know what her father did at work. Instead, he brought her to a conference. She was immediately taken by the atmosphere, the groups of men wearing lanyards indicating rank and company buzzing about. She kept seeing the same motif of job titles, director of this, associate director of that, assistant to the vice president of something else entirely. The convention center closed a few years later when the city began developing to the northwest. It had been Skyland Properties, the company run by Patrick Samson, that led the effort. What had once been a busy city was now a bustling metropolis thanks to them, or because of them depending on which way one looked at it.

As they exited the tunnel and Ana looked out at the abandoned convention center, she could see the sunset for the first time in years, unobstructed by the skyscrapers.

"If you're all some super elite accountants, why do you have to meet at a place like this? Why not a secret office or something?"

"Because we don't have any money."

She laughed out loud for more than a few moments, and only when she saw that Caldwell had remained expressionless did she realize that he was serious.

"I'm sorry, Mr. Caldwell. I didn't mean to be rude."

"Don't apologize, Ms. Leigh. I'm not a humous man, but even I can see the irony in accountants existing without accounts of their own."

They walked in silence for some time. Finally, Ana brought up Samson again in an effort to get Caldwell talking. He had promised to answer her questions, after all.

"When Patrick Samson died," Caldwell explained to Ana Leigh, "his estate was moved over to be managed by his successor, my client, who solicited my services to find all details relating to the financial discrepancies of Mr. Samson, all of which now point to the illegal mishandling of certain assets. Given that I cannot talk to Mr. Samson myself or persuade an answer from his colleagues, which would require the unique services of Mr. 4, I evoke the afterimage to lead me to the gaps in the ledger. It is a simple audit whichever way you look at it. I just happen to possess a very unique skill."

"Can you all summon images of the dead?"

Our man shook his head. "No, only me. The others have talents of their own. Mr. 3, for example, calls on the bodies of the dead, but they can provide no substantial information, just ears to listen with, mouths to report whispers, and hands to perform tasks. Mr. 1, on the other hand, deals more with the living, though once encountered, they tend to fall under the jurisdiction of myself or Mr. 3."

"He kills them?" Ana said, realizing more clearly the scope of these men, these accountants.

"He does more than that, Ms. Leigh, but I'll spare you the details. I have no intention of you encountering him at all. When we worked together as a five-man team this would have been simple, our talents combined meant absolute and thorough auditing."

"What happened?" Ana asked.

"Differences of opinion, office politics, homicide," Caldwell explained, "the usual. After the Enron collapse, when the Big Five became the Big Four, our superior, who, on paper, was an associate of Arthur Anderson LLC, made directives that were unsavory to some of us."

"... and you split up?"

"Just me. I left the group, but that doesn't mean I'm the only one who disagreed with our superior. Mr. 5 specializes in record-keeping and confided in me before I left. He said if I ever needed anything to come to him. I have recently discovered the undocumented payment of a substantial sum to someone whom I suspect to be the coroner Dr. James Kim. Right now, I need quick information on Dr. Kim and any links Samson had to him."

"Why not just talk to the police, report the issue."

"Why not indeed?" Caldwell said softly. "Two reasons, to be honest, which I strive to be at all times. First, because my client hired me to investigate outside of the parameters of the law and the public eye, and second, because the records that Mr. 5 possess cannot be found anywhere. He himself is a repository of knowledge. Everything that he has ever seen, heard, felt, or been told—he remembers. He can glance at records and imprint them in his mind. You can imagine how useful that can be in our line of work, I'm sure."

"Do you think he has information on Kim and Samson?"

"I know he does," said Caldwell as they approached the entrance of the convention center. "He knows about everyone. Every birth certificate, business registration form, passport application, and parking ticket that has ever seen the light of day is in Mr. 5's head, and not only does he remember each one, he is incredibly skilled at finding patterns and connecting the dots between them."

Caldwell took hold of the handle of a boarded-up glass door, pressed his foot against the wall, and pulled the door open, wooden boards clattered to the ground.

"We need to hurry. My former colleagues will be arriving at night. Mr. 5 always arrives early, and I intend to speak to him alone. This way, Ms. Leigh."

They walked at a fast pace through the long halls of the center. The building was all glass and steel structures curving overhead. Even in the utter state of disrepair the light of the setting sun made the interior look very beautiful. Ana could remember the hundreds of shoes marching from room to room, from booth to booth, and her father's hand around hers.

When the sound of shattering glass reverberated through the building, Ana, without thinking twice, took our man Caldwell by the hand.

"Let's go," said Caldwell, and they hastened their movement.

"I don't think so, Mr. 2," said a voice from above.

They looked up to see a man standing on a landing one floor above them, flanked by six or seven of the knife-brandishing hooded figures.

"I believe our superior will be happy to see his second in command again. Why don't you come with us?"

Ana looked at Caldwell, wondering if they should run. Caldwell shook his head, squeezing her hand in a silent gesture of reassurance. She remembered his words, that she was safe because she was under his protection. But she couldn't help wondering if he needed protection himself.

VIII

The hooded figures surrounded them as they were led by Mr. 3 down a long hallway, lit by a combination of gas lamps and the few remaining florescent bulbs that flickered rapidly, clinging to electric life.

At the end of the hall, Mr. 3 opened a door and ushered them into a large conference room where the table had been pushed up against the wall, the chairs stacked neatly in the corner. In the center of the room was a massive man wearing a suit that never seemed to be one color or another.

"Thank you, Mr. 3, for delivering our man, Mr. 2."

"You may call me Caldwell now, if you don't mind," Caldwell responded calmly.

The huge man turned slowly, revealing a face covered in a thick white and grey beard. "The Ledger has you as 2, and the Ledger is the only truth of this world until you die." His attention changed then, as did his tone. "Ms. Ana Leigh, I presume? It's a pleasure to meet you at last. Mr. 4 has told me all about you."

Ana said nothing.

"Where are you keeping Mr. 5?" said Caldwell.

"Shush. Now don't be rude. Ms. Leigh and I are having a conversation, aren't we miss?"

Ana remained silent. The giant Mr. 1 reached out and placed his hand on her chin, raising her gaze to meet his. His fingers smelled of blood and she couldn't help thinking how easily they could wrap almost entirely around her neck.

"Aren't we having a conversation, Ms. Leigh?" said Mr. 1 again.

"Why are your names numbers?" she asked.

"We're accountants, Ms. Leigh," said Mr. 1, "Numbers are all that we are."

"Now, Mr. 2—"

"*Caldwell*," said Caldwell.

Mr. 1 removed his hand from Ana's face and reached into his coat, drawing out two thick cigars, lighting one with a metal lighter and offering one out.

"Caldwell then," he said in a deep voice. "Won't you join me for a cigar—for old time's sake?"

"I quit," said Caldwell.

The giant chuckled. "The last time you said that to me was six years ago."

"Yes, and I also submitted it in writing. I am no longer bound to The Ledger Organization."

"And yet you are still bound to the Ledger itself," bellowed Mr. 1. He stomped across the room and lifted up a battered leather book. "You want freedom from this organization but want to keep your power and your life? Oh, my dear Caldwell, I'm afraid you cannot have it both ways. Come back to us or leave your power behind. Believe me when I say mortality won't suit you one bit."

Ana looked up at Caldwell, her eyes searching for answers that she would not get there in that room.

"Mr. 3, if you'd be so kind as to show our man Caldwell what you found?"

The small man placed a manila file in Caldwell's hand.

When Caldwell opened the file to look inside Ana could see that it was an autopsy report for Patrick Samson.

"We both know it would have been problematic for the public to find out that Dr. Kim used an un-identified body to double as Samson's. After all, if any-one really knew the truth then the circumstances of the merger would be called into question."

Caldwell examined the details of the file. Even Ana could see that the photo of the drowned body looked nothing like the man she had started at in the car.

"Your client must be the Glover Group then," said Caldwell, handing the file back over to Mr. 3.

"Indeed," said Mr. 1. "The Ledger Organization is about to regain our wealth and power."

Caldwell clenched his fist and stepped forward, "You can't possibly be thinking—"

Mr. 1 turned about more quickly than Ana sus-pected he was could and struck Caldwell square in the chest. Our man went flying across the room and hit the wall so hard that the drywall broke and Caldwell's back was lodged several feet up the wall for a moment before he fell to the ground.

Ana turned to run toward him, but the hands of the hooded figures were on her in an instant. She cried out, "Caldwell!"

She was amazed to watch him stand upright and dust himself off, but then she remembered how unfazed he had been after she hit him with her car. Still, he spoke as though he were in pain.

"You're really considering selling off the Ledger Organization?"

Mr. 1 took a deep drag from the cigar, the tip glowing red before being engulfed in smoke.

"On paper, we will be a subsidiary of the Glover Group, but make no mistake, the Ledger Organization lives on. I will not let the work of centuries fall apart, no matter how it looks on paper."

"What are you?" Ana whispered, but it was loud enough for Mr. 1 to hear.

"We have handled currency before currency was paper, before it was coin, before it was kept in vaults, and when the worth of a man was measured only by the number of sheep in his flock. We count and account and recount."

The words 'count and account and recount' were echoed by Mr. 3, in a deliberate and practiced manner.

Caldwell walked slowly across the room. "You're violating the work of your predecessors, Mr. 1."

"My predecessors are dead," the words flowed out and released a stream of smoke. "That is why I am 1, and why you are 2. Blood," he held up the leather ledger in his massive hand, "is the only currency of the world that remains constant."

"Where is Mr. 5?" Caldwell asked again slowly, eyes panning back and forth between Mr. 1 and Mr. 3. "Wherever you're keeping him, he won't give you any information that supports this insane endeavor, even Mr. 4 can't persuade that out of him."

"We know," said Mr. 3, "we already tried that."

"He had a very strong will," said Mr. 1.

Caldwell's eyes widened, and he sighed so heavily that his body seemed to deflate. "You can't mean that you killed him? He is the repository of centuries of knowledge, the record keeper, the historian. Tell me you didn't destroy that."

It was the first time Ana had witnessed genuine emotion in Caldwell's face. He became less of a statuesque entity and more of a man, and above all, in his eyes, he looked very old, older than his body, older than the entire city.

When nothing was said, Caldwell held out his hand and something like steam began to emanate from it. It flowed from his arm and collected on the ground, taking shape.

When the afterimage materialized, Ana was looking at a thin man with bright eyes and a light suit that was distressed and covered in dirt. The man was shaking his head, his lips pursed tightly, then turned around a run out of the room.

Caldwell darted out after the afterimage. Ana called out after him and wrenched herself from the grip of the hooded figures.

"Let them go," Mr. 1 said. Mr. 3 made a hand gesture and the bodies in hoods backed away.

Ana couldn't see where Caldwell had gone but she could hear his footsteps in the stairwell to her left. She ran in the direction of the sound and caught a glimpse of him turning a corner. Caldwell was gaining on the afterimage of Mr. 5 and Ana Leigh was gaining on Caldwell. Each hall led to another stairwell which led down to another floor, a repeating motif of lateral movement and descent underground. The halls became darker until only the glow of the afterimage illuminated their path.

Caldwell half tripped on an overturned table that must not have been there the day Mr. 5 was killed. Ana, close behind, managed to leap over it.

The afterimage vanished behind a door of green frosted glass. Caldwell, in full speed, rammed into the door with his shoulder and it came crashing down.

The room was a small office and the afterimage of Mr. 5 was hunched over the desk, a knife in his back, blood dripping down his white suit. Caldwell and Ana watched him slide off the desk.

She looked up at Caldwell, who watched in horror as entire worlds of knowledge died bleeding on the floor.

Again, without thinking twice, she took Caldwell by the hand.

"Don't you want to know what happens next?"

The voice of Mr. 1 came echoing down the dark hall behind them. One at a time, lights flickered along the corridor. Mr. 1 and Mr. 3 walked slowly toward them. Every few moments the lights would spark and go out and flicker on again, and the hulking form of Mr. 1 and his associate would appear a little closer to the threshold.

"Here, Mr. 2, I'll *show* you."

The lights flickered on again and Mr. 1 was right outside the doorway. Ana realized that Mr. 3 was no longer walking beside him, but was if fact being carried, held by the head, feet dangling inches off the ground, Mr. 1's hand was so large that his fingers wrapped around the 3's head and pinched down at the man's throat.

Before either of them knew what was happening Mr. 1 had Mr. 3 raised high in the air and was opening his mouth so wide that the sound of snapping jawbones was audible, and the massive man and his massive teeth took a notable chunk out of Mr. 3's side. A third of the man's width was now missing. His eyes were opened wide with pain but Mr. 1's grip was so tight that he could not scream. Mr. 1 did not chew, he bit and swallowed, flesh was immaterial, and bones insubstantial. Three bites and Mr. 3 had been divided in two. Six, and there was no torso left. He let go of the man's neck and dropped what remained of his upper half on the ground.

Caldwell was motionless. "What good does it do," he said, "to sell off the Ledger Organization if we are all dead."

Mr. 1's voice came out of a damp throat now, and his beard was red. "There were other 2's before you, Caldwell, and other 1's before me. New blood will be added to the Ledger. Mr. 3 made a mistake, and I cannot tolerate mistakes. But you, Mr. 2, have never made a mistake. Your resignation does not have to be permanent. We are about to become part of the Glover Group, and my client assures us that this will be a rebirth for us all."

Caldwell leaned in and whispered into Ana Leigh's ear.

She nodded and walked around the back of Mr. 1's desk. In the top drawer was a box of cigars. She pulled one out as instructed. On the desk, she noticed a familiar black card, Caldwell's, with a hole burned through it and a similar sized burn on the desk. There was a pile of burned papers that she recognized immediately as her own mail which had sat on the table in her condo.

Caldwell took the cigar from Ana and held it out to Mr. 1.

"Would you mind?"

Mr. 1 smiled and removed his lighter, igniting the end of the cigar as Caldwell drew short bursts of air through its length.

"Do you miss it, Mr. 2?" asked Mr. 1.

Caldwell exhaled smoke into the air between them and said, "Not at all. I left because I thought you were mad and were losing sight of what our organization was all about. Everything you've told me tonight is proof of that."

Like a dart, Caldwell expertly tossed the cigar through the air, landing the burning edge in the center Mr. 1's left eye. The man clapped a hand to his face and cried out, violently swinging the other hand around and making notable gouges in the doorway as he fell into it.

"You bastard, that hurts!"

Caldwell pulled the giant man by the shoulders so that he fell onto his front.

"Go!" shouted Caldwell.

Ana climbed over Mr. 1 and ran back out into the hall. As Mr. 1 began to climb to his feet, Caldwell closed his eyed and breathed calmly. His entire body began to radiate a white steam-like material. His breaths became deeper, and the glow around his body became thicker and more solid. When his eyes opened the entire room was filled with blinding light.

Mr. 1 focused his one undamaged eye and looked around frantically but could see only a mess of color and whiteness. A face or two would become visible and then a suit or a briefcase. He reached out to take hold of something, but his hand slipped straight through. He stood as tall has he could, taller than any person who had ever stepped foot in that office, over the heads of the hundreds of afterimages surrounding him. Caldwell was nowhere to be seen.

IX

Ana Leigh ran as fast as she could. Caldwell had told her to return to the room they had been brought to and to retrieve the Ledger. She retraced her steps, up stairs and down halls in a loop until she recognized the color of the carpet of the original floor.

She became abruptly aware of a person passing her, and then another a moment later. In seconds, the entire convention center was filled with people. Thousands of people shuffling from room to room, passing through one another, each sporting disparate suit styles. She had no idea that Caldwell could conjure up such a massive number of afterimages. Among them, it would be impossible for her to be noticed by anyone watching.

Ana found the room at the end of the hallway and was relieved to see that none of the hooded figures were there brandishing their knives. The Ledger sat at the table in the corner where Mr. 1 had picked it up. She lifted it and found that the leather book was significantly heavier than it looked.

None of the afterimages emitted any sound, and so Mr. 1's infuriated shouts emanated through the entire wing of the building.

Ana left the room and looked around, but there was no sign of Caldwell. She went down the main stairs to the entryway of the convention center where Caldwell had broken open the door. Looking around, it was clear there would be no way of picking him out among the crowd. She looked up and could see the afterimage of those who built the center, standing on nothing at all, hammering invisible nails into the highest reaches of the glass façade. She continued to scan her surroundings until she saw something familiar. A man with a face she recognized, standing with his arm extended and hand cupped as if holding the hand of a small child, but the child wasn't there. She was about to shout to the man, but she knew he wouldn't hear her.

Ana jumped when a hand touched her shoulder. She looked up to see Caldwell standing there.

"Come on, we have to get out of here. The building is going to collapse."

"What! Why?"

"Because sometimes an afterimage is transparent, and sometimes it is solid, and sometimes it is silent, and sometimes it has mass and weight. These," our man said, gesturing out, "have weight. Enough to bring down the entire building and, with any luck, Mr. 1 will still be lost inside it when that happens. Now let's go."

He took her by the hand and squeezed hard. She looked up at him and handed him the Ledger.

They didn't stop running until they were almost back at the tunnel. Ana's lungs were a heaving mess of pain and blood, her muscles numb with resistance.

The was a noise then, quieter than Ana would have expected, the groan of bending steel and shattering glass as the weight of the entire capacity of the convention center, hundreds of times over, brought down the building that had not been maintained for over a decade. A cloud of dirt erupted into the air, and the two ran through the tunnel.

They could see the black car that had driven them there, and the driver's door was open. Ana recognized

Caldwell's driver standing there, casually smoking a cigarette.

"Ms. Leigh, wait." Caldwell had stopped running.

She looked back at him and then at the driver, who was suddenly hunched over and clasping at his stomach, blood was dripping from his mouth and his mid-section. Ana ran up to him as he began to fall forward, but his body fell directly through her, casting a weight on her body from the inside out. She gasped as her lungs depressed and filed again.

Caldwell walked forward and placed a hand near the dead driver.

"I'm sorry, Mitch," he said, and the afterimage faded away. "It's 4, he's sending a message. That's why he left the car. *Shit*. Here, get in."

Caldwell took the wheel and Ana sat in the passenger seat.

He placed the ledger on her lap. "Open it. We need to know if Mr. 1 survived."

She pried open the book. Inside, the first pages were old, made of sheepskin or some similar material. As she flipped through, the pages seemed less worn down, each getting thinner, and stiffer, some had edges dipped in gold, and others were made of fabric. For every paged she tuned it seemed two more took its place. It was filled with names and numbers beside them. Most of the numbers had been crossed out and others written in a sequence. Each of the names seemed to be taken in black ink, but when the pages began to resemble more modern types, it was clear that they were written in blood, and with every turn of a page some of it cracked and fell apart.

"What is this?" she asked.

"Records," Caldwell responded. "Flip to the back."

She did so, the thin stack of pages feeling as though the was overturning a dictionary and found that the rear side of the final page was a heading written "Bookkeepers Present". There were a number of illegible signatures, many had been crossed out.

Caldwell glanced over and placed his finger on one of the stricken signatures.

"He's dead."

"Are you sure?"

Caldwell nodded looking back at the road. "I'm very sure. I've looked at that page for a long time. Besides, there are only two names left. One has to be Mr. 4."

"And the other's yours," Ana Leigh finished, shutting the book.

They drove back into the city and did not speak until it was clear Caldwell was driving them to Ana's building.

"So now what?"

"Well, Mr. 3 is dead, so he can't send his whisperers after you anymore. I think you're safe to go home. I need to give my report to my client."

"It's the middle of the night."

"And?"

Ana Leigh sighed as Caldwell pulled the car up to the building.

"Do you have anywhere to go?" she asked him, remembering that he was an accountant with no accounts.

He said nothing.

"I'd feel safer if you were with me tonight. You can stay the night and give your report in the morning."

"That's very kind of you to offer, Ms. Leigh, but I have to decline."

"No," she said, and Caldwell was taken aback. "You're my accountant, and as long as you have access to my accounts you work for me, right?"

Caldwell sighed and smiled, nodding.

"Well then this is what you need to do. I insist, and besides, it's your fault I got involved in all of this anyway."

Caldwell laughed for the first time in many years and shut off the car. "Very well, Ms. Leigh," he said, trying to sound exasperated.

They walked into the building and rode the elevator up to Ana's floor and entered her apartment.

"For the record," Caldwell said, shutting the door behind him, "if you hadn't hit me with your car, then you probably wouldn't have been involved."

She rolled her eyes and walked into the kitchen, peeling her shoes off and tossing them aside on the way. She grabbed one of the many gifted bottles of wine from her shelf and began to pour two glasses of white.

Ana watched Caldwell remove his coat and tie. It dawned on her that she had only ever seen him in a suit, and now that he was without it he seemed like a very different person.

She handed the glass of wine to him and walked back into her kitchen to look at the phone.

"Shit," she said.

"Is everything okay, Ms. Leigh?"

"Just twelve voicemails from work. I'd better go in tomorrow and make sure I still have a job."

"I hope you don't get into any trouble."

She took a long drink of wine and smiled. "It'll be okay. Edwards is a prick, but he wants to fuck me so bad I'm sure he'll let it slide."

Caldwell awkwardly shifted his eyes and sipped from the glass, taking a seat at her dining room table.

"Oh, I'm sorry. It's been a long day." She sat across from him at the small table. "So, have you ever been with anyone?"

He nodded. "I had a wife once, but she died a long time ago. After that it seemed better to remain alone."

"So, you really are…"

"Immortal?" he said calmly. "Yes, as far as aging is concerned. But we can be killed, as tonight has so vividly illustrated."

"Vivid is right," Ana said, taking another long drink and trying not to replay all the events of the past few hours. "So, what do you think happened with Samson? I mean, what are you going to tell your client?"

"I believe that Samson was being strong-armed to merge Skyland with the Glover Group. It was really more of an acquisition than a merger. Doing so would give the Glover Group total control over the city's planning and development. But Samson was a prideful man. He didn't want his company to be absorbed like that, especially after all the work he did transforming this city. But somebody had something on him, and I'm convinced he was smuggling money out of Korea for Dr. Kim.

"In exchange, Dr. Kim would provide the body necessary for Samson to fake is own death. If the only thing forcing the merger was whatever the Glover Group had on him, then he could easily leave instructions to his vice president to end the conversation and to take over the company after his death. He was the kind of man who would run away and start a new life if it meant ensuring his legacy remained. I suppose I can empathize. I've started a dozen new lives at least."

Ana watched him finish his first glass, and she got up to replenish both of their drinks.

"But Samson died, and the merger happened anyway," she said.

"That's correct, and the turning point was the moment that you witnessed in the car the other day. Mr. 4 is a master of persuasion, and Mr. 1 is, well, intimidating to say the least. I believe Samson was threatened into going forward with the arrangement he made with Kim but was forced to authorize the merger. After that, Mr. 1… 'disposed' of Patrick Samson."

"But it seems strange for the Ledger Organization to get involved."

"We're hired guns these days, Ms. Leigh. We work for whoever offers the work."

"You can call me Ana."

He thanked her for the second glass of wine and avoided using her name entirely, the attempt at informality failing him.

"At any rate," he continued, "once Mr. 1 expressed that the Ledger Organization would become subservient to the Glover Group it all made sense. The delivery of Samson to the Glover Group was just a show of good faith. Whoever is pulling the strings knows a lot more than any person I've met in modern history."

"What do you mean?"

"Well, they know about us, about the Ledger Organization—and our talents."

Ana nodded, and, emboldened by drink, placed her hand on top of Caldwell's. He looked down at her hand and place his other hand over it, slowly caressing her wrist with his fingertips.

"You should get some sleep, Ana. You've got to get to work in the morning." He pulled his hand away and took her empty glass into the kitchen and began to rinse it in the sink.

"Goodnight, Caldwell," she said walking into her bedroom, wondering if she heard him over the running water.

X

The morning sun came streaming through the blinds, casting stripes of light across her. Ana could see that it was morning before she opened her eyes. It felt like every other morning, the faint pounding in her temples a reminder of the previous night's wine, and her hair tangled and twisted under her head. She wondered if everything had just been a dream, but that thought faded quickly.

She emerged to find Caldwell still asleep on her couch, his suit coat acting as a blanket. Despite his resolve, the events of the previous days exhausted him, and she wondered how long it had been since he last slept. Had it been days? Or do immortal accountants go months without sleeping? She certainly knew accountants who could go a few days, and they often boasted about it, as if sleep deprivation was a badge of honor to be worn about the workplace.

Caldwell was still fast asleep after Ana had showered and dressed for work. She left him there and went down to the garage feeling much more inclined to drive to work, rather than take her chances walking on her own again. Still, she felt safer that day than any other day, a feeling of resolution surrounding her and the man who was still sleeping in her apartment. Before climbing in, she walked to the front of her car and placed a hand over the dent on the hood.

He was right; none of it would have happened if she had not hit him with her car. She smiled, glad for the first time in her life to have been in a car accident.

She arrived at work to find her desk wholly unperturbed save for a small pile of accumulated mail. They were mostly solicitations for printing companies and other vendors looking to be hired by the agency, a thank you card from a former client among them, and several memos from Human Resources describing nuanced changes to company policies.

What on earth was she doing with her life? She always knew that she had no love for her job, but at that moment she could confidently say that she outright hated it. Tossing the pile of mail into the trash basket under her desk, she grabbed her purse and placed it on her lap.

She could just leave and not come back, Ana thought, how bad could that be?

There was a figure above the divider of her desk.

"How nice of you to show up." It was Edwards, looking slightly annoyed, but mostly pleased with himself, as usual. "Do you have anything for me?"

"What are you talking about, Edwards?"

"The reports that I asked you for. They're three days late. I suppose this means you haven't listened to any of my voicemails. Where the hell have you been?"

Ana sighed, "Look, Edwards, I'm sorry. I haven't been feeling well and some things came up so—"

"What kind of things?" he asked in his most patronizing voice.

"Just things, okay. I'll get caught up. Just let me get back to work."

Edwards folded his arms on the divider wall and rested his chin down, staring at her. "I think it would be best if you tell me where you've been."

"Edwards, with all due respect, *buzz off.*" She was done being polite, though her drive to just up and quit her job was quickly diminishing, the reality of her work and life dissipated the fantasy.

"Ana, don't you want to *tell me where you've been?*" Edwards' voice became slow and rhythmic. She stared up at him, his smile wide.

"I've been with a friend," she said.

"Tell me about him."

"It's really not important, Edwards. He's a friend from outside of work."

"I would love to hear all about him, Ana. *Tell me where he is. Tell me where he's going. Tell me where to find him. Take me to Caldwell.*"

XI

Our man Caldwell sat in the lobby outside the office of Liam Nguyen, the president of Skyland Properties, or at least what was left of it after the acquisition by the Glover Group. He recalled his initial meeting with Nguyen, in which the man asked him to investigate the discrepancies in his predecessor's accounts. Nguyen had seemed concerned that any mishandling could cause trouble for him in his new role, or the new incarnation of his company. There were more buildings to build, cities to erect, lands to conquer, and the resources of the powerful Glover Group were behind him now make it all happen. He would have nothing so insubstantial as the past interfere with his trajectory.

It was clear that Nguyen was methodical and pragmatic. He never once mentioned to Caldwell the death of Patrick Samson, who had once been his superior, nor did he allude to any sort of foul-play. Caldwell had gone a great deal of time without work, without a project, and he doubted very much that Nguyen would elicit his unique services had he not suspected such activities—the overtones resonating by the situation and requiring no explicit acknowledgement. The prospect of work and the intrigue of the situation made it impossible for Caldwell to decline.

As with all audits, this one had come to a close, and while the work itself made Caldwell feel alive, it was the conclusion, the neat packaging of a report that made him feel whole.

There was no report to give in writing this time. Caldwell made the decision that a verbal testimony of his findings would not only suffice for Nguyen, they would be preferred.

"Mr. Nguyen is ready for you, sir."

Caldwell stood and let himself into the office. There, Nguyen stood the window, staring at his inherited city like a temple guardian from a bygone age.

"Welcome back, Mr. Caldwell. Please have a seat."

"I'll stand thanks. I doubt this will take very long."

Liam Nguyen turned and looked Caldwell up and down. "I take it that there is nothing to report, given that you are empty-handed." Nguyen spoke English the same way Caldwell did, perfectly, yet unable to fully hide the melody of some distant homeland.

"Not exactly," Caldwell replied, "rather, I thought it best my findings should not be in writing."

"Very well then, I'm listening. But before you begin I'll warn you that I have a guest arriving soon. Please forgive me if I have to cut your report short."

Caldwell wondered who Nguyen might be expecting during the workday, especially someone with whom he would refer to as a guest. He nodded assent.

"All I had to go on when we spoke was your description of Samson's calls; the calls made to you and his wife before he died. Everything else was so neat. The media played the merger out as though the decision was yours alone, and the result of Samson's death."

Nguyen raised his eyebrows. "Which is how I wish it to remain. Of course, when I found discrepancies with our internal reports, it was clear that I needed someone like you, an external auditor to investigate. So what did you find?"

"Through my methods," Caldwell continued, "I was able to discover that Patrick Samson made a hasty visit to the coroner Dr. James Kim several days before his death. In addition, just two days before he was reportedly discovered in the bay, he had a five-minute conversation with someone or perhaps more than one person in a car parked just outside of a café not far from his home."

"Mr. Caldwell, I believe you were hired to investigate Patrick's accounts, not the accounts of his death."

Caldwell walked a few steps further into the office. "But the two are inherently related, Mr. Nguyen, and I am very thorough."

Nguyen considered this for a moment and then nodded. "But how did you know about this conversation in a car?"

"Samson was a creature of habit," Caldwell explained, "he took the same path to work every day. On his days off, he rarely stayed home, and would walk to one of the few restaurants in the same area as this building, deviating as little as possible from his usual route. I suspected that any deviation would give me insight to any anomalies in his life, financial or otherwise. Irregularities are highly conspicuous when involving regular people.

"Again, through my methods I was able to observe his movements day after day until I found the first discrepancy, in which he ran, not walked, and took an alternate route, ending up at Dr. Kim's clinic. The next day, his route was altered again. He stood on the sidewalk and waited for some time, then entered a vehicle for about five minutes and got out again, at which point he made the calls to you and his wife."

Nguyen walked over to his desk, lifted a glass of water to his lips and sipped. "I still don't see how this is related to Patrick's mishandling of Skyland's finances."

Caldwell raised a hand. "Ah yes, let me explain. Dr. Kim was the clue. The best way to discover the details of a discrepancy is to compare one ledger to another. It would have been no good for me to simply pour over Skyland's accounts, so I instead chose to investigate Kim's. That's where I found it—income discrepancies. His profits to the clinic didn't add up, and remarkably, the extra income matched up perfectly with Skyland's missing funds in both quantity and timeline."

"I see, very good Mr. Caldwell." Nguyen did not seem genuinely impressed, but Caldwell did not look for such affirmation. He looked only for the truth that always hid itself away in the details and the numbers.

"Now I have a question for you, Mr. Nguyen."

Nguyen was unperturbed. "Oh?" was all he said.

"It's clear that Patrick Samson was funneling money to James Kim, whose clinic was little more than a front to allow him to regain control of his Korean assets. I think if you were to look into it you would find a number of investments in South Korea, acquired properties if I were to guess, which would account for the discrepancies you discovered after becoming President and CEO."

"And your question, Mr. Caldwell?"

"You were the CFO before all of this happened. How is it that you found the discrepancies only after Samson died?"

Nguyen smiled then. "Very good, Mr. Caldwell. You've lived up to everybody's expectations." He pressed his finger to a button on the phone sitting on the desk and spoke down into it. "Please show our guests in."

The office door opened, and Caldwell turned to see Ana Leigh accompanied by a man with cropped blonde hair.

"Ms. Leigh, and Mr. Edwards," said Nguyen, "Please shut the door behind you."

"It's good to see you again, Mr. 2," said Edwards.

"I wish I could say the same, Mr. 4," replied Caldwell. "Ana, are you alright?"

She seemed to be unharmed, and Caldwell assumed as much since Mr. 4 was not one to take the physical approach, especially when his former superior was so adept in that particular brand of persuasion.

Mr. 4 used words, and it was clear from the look on Ana Leigh's face that she was just realizing what sort of trick of the mind had been played on her.

"I knew you'd be here," she said slowly, "and he asked me to bring him to you. Edwards, he asked…and I brought him. Why?"

"It's fine, Ana. My former colleague is gifted in the art of persuasion."

Mr. 4 looked at Caldwell with a big smile. "I suppose," he began, "I should call you 'Mr. 1' now."

"You can call me Caldwell, and then you can leave."

Mr. 4 laughed, his perfect teeth spreading just a little too far apart, and eyes opening uncomfortably wide. "You've finally developed a sense of humor. It's too bad it came at the end of your eternal career."

Nguyen drew a pistol from his desk, holding it by the barrel, and held it out as he walked towards Mr. 4.

"You see," Mr. 4 said. "I could never have killed our superior myself, but now that you have done the work for me I'm about to become the head of the Ledger Group. I think this will be the first time that a 4 has become a 1 in such a short period of time."

It was clear then that Nguyen was the one pulling the strings on behalf of the Glover Group. He had employed both Mr. 4 and Caldwell himself for separate purposes to the same end: Caldwell to find the blind spots, and Mr. 4 to tie up the loose ends then take over. Or perhaps Mr. 4 had used his talent to persuade Nguyen into this entire course of action, but Caldwell found that unlikely; 4 had never been a planner. It didn't matter in the least, because as Mr. 4 reached out to receive the pistol from Nguyen's hand, the man instead used the back of the gun to strike Mr. 4 in the jaw. As the accountant stumbled back, Nguyen flipped the pistol in his hand and shot Mr. 4 square in the face.

Ana gasped, watching the body fall, and stepped back as it hit the ground.

"Well," Nguyen said, placing the pistol in his back pocket, "that's done. Now, where were we?"

Caldwell stared down at the body of his last colleague. He had been no friend of Mr. 4, but the feeling of loneliness that his work had always kept at bay flooded in as quickly and violently as the dark, ink-colored fluid pouring from Mr. 4's head.

"What's the point?" Caldwell asked. "Honestly, I don't think you really needed me to find out anything about Patrick Samson. It can't be that you just want us all dead. Why the charade?"

"It was you," Ana said, putting together what Caldwell had already assumed. "You're the one who was blackmailing Samson, you're the one representing the Glover Group."

"Correct, Ms. Leigh," Nguyen replied, "I can see why our man Caldwell has taken a liking to you. But you're both operating under false assumptions. I knew about Kim, and I knew about Mr. 4's ambition, but it was really *you* we wanted all along, Mr. Caldwell. You are now the sole proprietor of the Ledger Organization and we are prepared to offer you a substantial—"

Caldwell raised his hand. "I don't want your money. The Ledger is not for sale."

Nguyen placed a hand on his heart apologetically. "You misunderstand me. I was going to say that we are prepared to offer you a substantial *opportunity*. You will sit on the Board of the Glover Group itself and oversee the accounts of all of the other board members. It's a job, no matter which way you look at it, and one in which you can keep a group of men accountable. It can be risky when people in power are plagued with scandal."

"This was just some kind of test?" Ana glanced back and forth between Nguyen and Caldwell hoping one would make the situation somewhat more meaningful considering she had just witnessed a murder.

Nguyen smiled. "What do you say, Mr. Caldwell? Will you join us? The circles of my employer are filled with men whose lives are rife with ignominy, and it will be critical to keep their accounts recorded and their actions supervised. The Ledger will remain yours, and my employer wants to ensure you that it will remain that way. There is enough ancient magic in Mr. Alice's pocket—your ledger is of no concern. This has all been an interview, to your point, Ms. Leigh, and our man here has passed with flying colors."

"Was it your intention that the others end up dead?" asked Caldwell. "So that I would be the one to accept or decline the post?"

"You saw what became of Mr. 1," said Liam Nguyen. "He was willing to sell off the Ledger to keep his little organization alive. Samson was the same. No vision or purpose, just a perpetuation of self-interest. I watched as Patrick Samson walked the fool's path, making decisions for his own benefit that would lead this company into ruin. He was short-sighted, always chasing the next small conquest instead of looking at the part he played in the greater drama.

"We have always been subservient to the Glover Group, just never on paper.

"Mr. 1 served his purpose, granting the Glover Group a great deal of additional power and influence, and demonstrating how single-minded he was. But the group is not after single-mindedness. You're a much more reasonable man. Think about it; you don't have to be a hired gun anymore, Mr. Caldwell. You can be the bookkeeper for the world's currency. Isn't that what you were always meant to do?"

Caldwell held the Ledger tight in his hands.

"What about Mr. 5," Caldwell asked through his teeth. "Everything he knew is lost now. He was the record keeper."

"Yes, that was a tragedy, and an unexpected one. We had hoped he would assist you. The man never had a desire to lead, which is why he remained 5, but Mr. 1 proved to be more of a wild card than any of us expected. Killing Mr. 5 simply served to strengthen our resolve that you take over."

"Mr. 1 is wildness incarnate, Mr. Nguyen. You should do your research before playing with explosives. Mr. 5's death might have been prevented."

"I concede on that point, Mr. Caldwell. But war always leaves casualties. I know you've seen a few wars yourself, but are you going to spend the rest of your long life dwelling on the past or helping to carve the future?"

"I don't feel inclined to do you any favors."

"I can understand that." Nguyen walked back to the desk and settled into his seat, looking out the wide window in thought. Finally, he offered an alternative. "Why don't you take some time to think about it? My assistant will have all of the files on the members of the

Board sent to you. Look through them, and I'll be in touch."

The door to the office opened behind them.

"The choice is yours, Mr. Caldwell. Nobody will force you. But rest assured that you will be taken care of if you agree to this. Enjoy the rest of your day, and Ms. Leigh, it was a pleasure to meet you.

Ana and Caldwell had to step over the body of Mr. 4 to exit the office.

XII

Caldwell perused the files one at a time. They were spread over the length of Ana Leigh's dining room table. The more he read, the more his head shook.

"Is it bad?" Ana asked.

"These *people*," he said, amazed. "It's a mess. And from the look of it, the mess is growing. This group is getting more and more powerful, and the kind of waste and scandal is appalling. There's even a file on Patrick Samson. It looks like Nguyen was blackmailing Samson for using a property for some sex trafficking operation. I don't approve of Nguyen's actions, but I can hardly blame him for wanting Samson out of the picture. He was a liability, plain and simple."

"He didn't have to murder him though. He could have turned him in."

"No," Caldwell said. "It would have destroyed the company. Samson's finances were too embroiled with Skyland's."

Ana regarded the way Caldwell's judgements were always objective, and never moral. Mr. 5's death was the only thing that had struck him, but she conceded that it was his knowledge that Caldwell added value to, not the man, and the careless loss of that value affected him as an accountant. She wondered how much of him was still human.

"But look here," Caldwell continued, "one of the board members solicited from the trafficking operation, and he even owns residences in several Skyland buildings. His name is Jack Orsen, and he was the former CFO of Vault Prosthetics, which was quietly absorbed by the Glover Group just a few months ago."

"So what are you thinking?" Ana asked.

"I'm thinking that I don't like being manipulated," Caldwell responded.

"Yeah I get that."

"I'm also thinking that I've never seen this much fiscal irresponsibility and such a magnitude of wealth all concentrated in one place. Nguyen was right, the fact that the group now controls so many resources on paper means nothing. They control the currency."

Ana could see the light glisten in his eyes. "Listen," she said. "I don't know a lot about this world of yours, but it sounds like this is a job that only you can do. If you don't do it, what else will you do?"

Caldwell had never been faced with that question. He had been just one thing all his life. There was a time that only Mr. 5 would have remembered, when the Ledger Organization had a purpose and a destiny—but unfulfilled destinies are destinies nonetheless, and the Ledger Organization's bookkeepers had lost sight of it a long time ago. Perhaps this was the moment to redefine his purpose, now that he was alone.

As if reading his mind, Ana Leigh put into words just what he had been contemplating. She said,

"Caldwell, you left the Ledger Group because Mr. 1 was doing things you didn't like. Maybe this is your chance to fix it? Make the right decisions."

She placed her hand on his shoulder and used her thumb to caress his neck. He placed his hand on hers and stopped her. "Ana, listen…"

"Wait," she said, and walked out of the room. After a moment she returned with a folded sheet of paper in her hand. "Before you say anything, I wanted to give you this."

He took the sheet from her and opened it. "What is this?" he asked.

"You said that I could fire you at any time, but that it would have to be in writing. Well, here it is. I'm officially dissolving our professional relationship. You are no longer authorized to administer my accounts, and I am no longer under your protection."

He wasn't certain exactly how he felt about it. 'Disappointment' was the word that kept appearing in his mind.

She wrapped her arms around him and whispered in his ear. "Yeah, that's the look I had when I first got off the phone with you. There's a reason I never called back about fixing the car."

He turned to look at her, and their faces were almost touching.

"I suppose," he said slowly. "We don't necessarily need a professional reason to be in contact. After what you've been through I suppose it is only natural for us to remain in touch."

She smiled and ran her fingers through his hair. "Yeah, I think that makes sense. But if you didn't agree I could have just held the car damage over your head for the rest of your life."

"I still intend to pay for that, Ms. Leigh."

"How were you going to pay for it in the first place? You don't have any money."

"Well I had hoped this Samson audit would have taken care of that."

Ana shifted her body and wrapped her leg around the chair, straddling Caldwell and remaining face to face. She lifted one of the files from the table and held it up.

"So, it sounds like you're in need of a job."

"And so are you, Ms. Leigh."

"We could make a good team," she replied, placing a hand on his chest. An aspect came about her that he had been ignorant of, *ambition* and competence that he had dismissed the moment she struck him with her car. He had made such errors before.

He took her hand in his. "We can't be a team forever. Everything in this world is temporary."

"I know," she said. "But I don't care. The last few days have been much more exciting than marketing will ever be. Temporary is fine. Eternity wouldn't suit me."

She stood up and dimmed the lights while Caldwell removed his coat and tossed it on the chair. "Goodnight, Mr. Caldwell."

"Goodnight, Ms. Leigh," our man replied as she walked off into her room. He sat and, after many hours of contemplation and calculation, rested his head on the arm of the sofa and closed his eyes.

Curio Case, Cloakroom, & **Conclusion**

Boardrooms have personalities all their own. They hold people who hold power, who make decisions on behalf of others—and the walls of boardrooms hold secrets, none more so than the true nature of the individuals who sit within them. If these rooms were sentient creatures they might find themselves brimming with tears, reeling with images of the corrupt—but, most likely, they'd be bored out of their wits. Meeting after meeting layering contentious discussions on petty office politics sandwiched between world-changing corporate governance and the union of alphas, egos, and god-knows what else. In this case, god is in the drywall.

Penny, the assistant to board member Nils Glass took the collated and stapled packets of letter-size pages containing agendas, reference documents, and presentation bullets from the printer to her desk where she slipped them each into monogramed black leather folders, stacked them onto a cart, and wheeled them into the boardroom located on the 43rd floor of the Glover

Group main headquarters. She set each folder in its proper place on the table, ensuring the placement of every board member was such that those who needed to face one another were facing one another, those who needed to be adjacent were adjacent, and those who sat at the heads of the table did, in fact, sit at the heads. She paused for a moment and smiled as she placed her own direct superior's folder down on the table and slipped a small piece of paper she had torn from her personal notebook under the cover. She'd been fucking him for ages and liked to tease him. She let her fingers glide over the silver initials **NG** before carrying on with arranging the refreshments on a side table. The gin in the glass bottle had been refreshed in such a way that it appeared just empty enough to be inviting but filled enough to be ample for the enjoyment of the members expected to be present given the precise accounts of each individual's drinking habits, their vices calculated with precision.

The room was left in silence for twenty minutes before the sound of shuffling shoes brought the board-room to life.

Two men walked in together.

"I expect he'll call it a manageable mishap but'll be pissing himself on the inside. He doesn't like when mistakes at that level need to be cleaned up," said the first man, taking a deep drag from a cigarette and exhaling a cloud of grey smoke.

"You really ought to stop smoking those things, Orsen. Clean air is hard enough to come by without your help."

Orsen shrugged and tossed the cigarette into an empty metal wastepaper basket, leaving it lit so that a single tendril of smoke rose and curled and dissipated over the next several minutes.

"Tell you what, if he hasn't brought it up by the time the smoke stops," Orsen offered, "I'll knock over a glass of bourbon and use it as an excuse to change the subject. What do you say?"

The other man, smaller and with softer facial features found his initials JzV on a folder and took a seat. "I think they usually have gin at these things, Orsen."

Orsen walked over and lifted up the decanter, sniffed it, then poured himself a glass. "Fine. All I'm saying is that he's been skirting the issue for too long. *Guarantee* it isn't on the agenda. Shit, they've always got me sitting next to you, Zoë. How the hell am I supposed to make dramatic glances over to you when I hear the bullshit coming out of their mouths?"

"I don't think it matters," Vault responded. "Who's that over there?" He gestured to the seat opposite them.

Orsen picked it up and took a sip of his drink. "It's **HC**. Who the hell is that?"

"It's Hail. Here switch them around. He usually takes the minutes, so I'll be able to glance over at his computer and check the time. They don't put clocks in here."

Orsen handed the folder to Vault and took a seat across from them.

"Morning, Nils." Vault said, observing the slender man entering the room, unwinding a brown plaid scarf from around his neck.

"Morning, Vault. Orsen."

Orsen nodded and tapped his glass on the wooden table.

Nils Glass took his seat at the table and promptly opened his folder to review the meeting's agenda. Vault watched him lift a small piece of paper and promptly crumple it, slipping it into his pocket as a flush came over his face.

Three men entered within a few minutes and another two trickled in moments before 10:00am. All but three seats were filled in the room by the time the meeting began.

They all sat in silence until Hail Counterpart, noting the time on his computer screen looked around and began to take roll of present members of the Glover Group's Board of Directors.

Present:
Glass
Vault
Orsen
Counterpart
Caldwell
Coin

Absent:
Alice, *Ex Officio*
Smith
Fletcher

"Anybody heard from Fletcher?" said Coin.

A rumbling and shaking of heads.

Counterpart looked up from his computer, "He has failed to send me any communications despite my emails. I suspect he is indisposed or away on an emergency."

"That man lives in another dimension, I swear," said Coin.

"At any rate, the election of a new Co-Chair needs to commence before any business can begin," Counterpoint stammered. "Do I hear any nominations?" His fingers rested on his keys, at the ready.

The men looked around at one another.

"It should be Caldwell," said Vault. "He's got the best fiduciary acumen, the only accountant among us."

Glass nodded, "I agree. That seems reasonable."

Caldwell silently surveyed the room, then nodded assent.

"Very well," said Counterpart, "all in favor?"

The vote was unanimous.

Caldwell stood from his seat and walked around to the head of the table. The other head was empty as always, in the absence of Mr. Alice, who had never been physically present at any meeting of the Glover Group's Board of Directors.

"Our man, Caldwell," muttered Coin.

Caldwell did not speak for some time. He opened the leather folder and removed the papers inside, eyes scanning the pages methodically and efficiently.

At last, he said, "The first item on the agenda—"

The startling sound of a glass toppling and the splashing of gin interrupted the new co-chairman.

"Christ," Vault said under his breath, rolling his eyes at Orsen.

Orsen sat there awkwardly before picking up the glass and standing. He moved back to the decanter and replenished his drink.

"Well speaking of finances," Orsen said casually, "there's the matter of cost-of living adjustments for the employees of our clinics."

"No," said Caldwell.

Orsen's attempt and nonchalance faltered, and he gave Caldwell a sharp look.

"Two points," Caldwell began, "the first: your request has not been properly agendized. The second, all subsidiary entities of the Glover Group have a flat COLA annually, no exceptions, and besides, your clinics no longer exist as far as the rest of the world is concerned."

"Yes, we understand that," said Vault, "but the flat rate relates only to the employees who had their jobs replaced by automatons. That decision was made years ago and didn't account for the, erm, *acquisitions* that Mr. Alice would make after taking over. These are experts and engineers, and we'll lose them if we aren't competitive."

"Mr. Vault."

"We've done everything on our side as instructed, but my team are some of the best in the—"

"Mr. Vault," Caldwell said again with a slight shift in volume. "*The agenda.*"

Vault nodded and Orsen took his seat again.

"Now," said Caldwell. "Top of the agenda would be how to handle the growing tensions between the Director of Development and the Director of Expansion."

"They're having a pissing contest," said Coin. "Why do we need to intervene."

"I'll remind everyone," said Counterpart, looking up from his computer, "that the Director of Expansion has a pending request for funding an expedition as well as a unique asset transfer. It was tabled at the last meeting." Counterpart returned to typing.

"Thank you for the reminder," said Caldwell.

"Remind me what she's doing again?" asked Glass.

Vault, removed a document from the folder. "She's trying to send a man to Mars, and she would like a seed from the Tree of Life I believe."

"Ah, that's right."

"I mean," Coin spoke up, "we could just let her do it. I don't see the harm."

"If we do that," Vault began, "acquire the seed, that is, then the Director of Development will expect it. I hear he hasn't had much luck with the accelerated evolution project."

"That guy kills kids," Orsen said sharply. "I say we defund him altogether."

"Is that a motion?" said Counterpart.

Orsen shrugged.

"There is a motion to grant the aforementioned request to the Director of Expansion and to withdraw funding from the Department of Development."

"Second," said Coin.

"All in favor?" Caldwell ordered, then glanced around, acknowledging the raised hands, all were raised except for Nils Glass, who seemed to be struggling to decide his opinion. "The motion is carried. Next, is…"

Caldwell paused.

"…the resolution to dissolve the Ledger organization and prohibit the addition of new names to the Ledger itself, prohibiting the endowment of talents and eternal life to any individual not already recorded. It goes without saying" he said, flipping his folio closed, "that I will recuse myself from this vote."

The group looked around at one another.

"I just received an email," said Counterpart. "Mr. Alice has an opinion on this."

"Then is there a point of even discussing it?" This was Vault. Orsen hummed in agreement.

"He has concerns with the talents of the individual previously known as Mr. 5, and warns against creating a new repository of knowledge."

Caldwell stood. "This decision will be postponed."

"Caldwell," said Counterpoint, "I don't think that would be wise."

"If Mr. Alice wants to talk about it then I expect him at the next board meeting. This meeting is adjourned."

They all stood as Caldwell left the room.

Orsen sipped his drink and clapped Vault on the shoulder. "Well that went well."

"Next time, just put it on the agenda," Vault said, taking the drink from Orsen's hand and slamming it on the table. "Oh and 'that guy kills kids' might be a little heavy handed for you. You're no saint yourself. How's your daughter?"

Orsen went pale. "Do you think Caldwell knows?"

"I think he knows everything," Vault said in a hushed tone. "I heard he has tabs on all of us."

"Hail," said Glass from across the room, "Sam and I are having some folks over tomorrow night. You interested?"

"No thank you, Nils," said Counterpoint, "I'm looking forward to my weekend. Going to find a nice spot to catch up on some work, I think."

"Suit yourself, maybe I can try to get ahold of Alistair. He hasn't answered his phone in days."

"Very strange."

"Nils," said Vault, "you think Caldwell is okay?"

Glass shrugged. "I can never tell with that guy. I guess we'll find out next time."

"We'll wait and see," said Orsen.

They shook hands and waived one another away, leaving the boardroom as silent as it had been that morning. The air had a lingering odor of spilled gin and well-ordered smugness as dry as the alcohol.

Penny collected the discarded agendas and leather folders. The folders were placed on a cart for reuse, and the agendas and documents she brought with her to the incinerator down the hall, saving only the note that Glass had left for her and slipping it into her pocket before returning to the staff cloakroom.

During Board meetings, it was important for the staff to be readily available. In the beginning, they would be called on often to perform tasks, retrieve data, or simply fetch lunch. After the Board worked itself into a rhythm, these tasks became less frequent. The cloakroom was old—easily the oldest room in the building. It was at the absolute center of the tower where the Glover Group met and had become the central headquarters of a number of companies under the group's control, including Vault Prosthetics, Skyland Properties, and the Ledger Organization. The building had been expanded several times, and the outermost offices were modern and sleek in contrast to the center. The walls were cascading layers of glass in many areas. Each layer had once been the outermost, had once had a direct view to the city outside, but now looked out at a newer office and a newer one yet beyond, each a timestamp of architecture and décor, forming windows to the past and future. The existence of a cloakroom was a vivid reminder of the history of the building.

Penny wheeled the cart with the stacks of folders and glasses atop it.

Stephan, another assistant, looked up from a document he had been skimming. "I heard a crash. Did somebody start throwing things again?"

"No," Penny sighed, "but your boss spilled gin all over the table."

"Was it Vault or Orsen?"

"Which do you think?"

Stephan resumed skimming the text on his lap. "Right, Orsen then."

A knock at the door.

Penny opened it to reveal a man they had never seen on that level of the building before. He was a skinny man standing in the doorway, dressed in an old suit.

"Afternoon," the man said in a thick London accent. "Might I inquire as to which of you reports to Mr. Caldwell?

"That's me," Ana Leigh said, standing from her position at the back of the room.

"Very good," said the man. He produced an envelope from his breast pocket and handed it over to her. "Please see that this gets to him, and by this evening if possible. It is for Mr. Caldwell's eyes only. I can trust you'll deliver it?"

Ana nodded.

"That's all then," said the man politely. "Cheers," and he was gone.

A few minutes later, Nils Glass poked his head in just as penny had finished unloading the cart.

"Penny," he said. "Sam just left me a message, I've got to go."

"*Shit*," said Penny, and Stephan made a kind of whistling noise in an I-told-you-so sort of tone.

"It's fine," said Glass. "Just take care of the rest of the work today, don't send me any calls and, obviously, don't call yourself."

"We'll talk tomorrow," said Penny. Of course, they would not, because Nils Glass would be in a coma with a gunshot wound within the hour. But that story has already been told.

Vault caught Caldwell as he was packing up to leave the building, his coat and hat already on. Caldwell was filling his briefcase with stacks of papers from his desk, which he stowed away more hastily when he noticed Vault in his doorway.

"Caldwell," Vault began. "I wanted to talk about the meeting. I'm sorry for being so abrupt, but the well-being of my employees is important to me. Many of my engineers are patients themselves and their medical costs are quite extraordinary."

"You were not abrupt," Caldwell replied. "You were simply out of order. I've already put your concerns at the top of next week's agenda."

Vault stepped a little further into the man's office and Caldwell, seeing that there was more to the conversation than the agenda of the Board of Directors, offered for him to take a seat.

"This whole thing has just been hard for me," said Vault. "You seem to be handling it very well even though you've barely just arrived."

"Mr. Vault, you've spent your life committed to serving others," Caldwell began, attempting to sound conciliatory. "But the business of service and the business of business can often have conflicting needs. I've been on both sides, and this group is nothing more than a manifestation of what has always existed. The Glover Group is just the form that this century's regime has taken. It's not the worst that has ever been, and it won't be the last that history sees."

"But history doesn't *see* it at all. That's the point. None of this is right, these world-altering decisions being made in secret. The seed of the tree of life, accelerated evolution, the management of international economies as though they were rainy-day savings accounts."

Caldwell looked over his shoulder and closed the office door before asking, "Can I ask why you're coming to me with this, Mr. Vault?"

Vault glanced over at Caldwell's desk. "I know you have dirt on all of us. They brought you in to make sure nobody does anything stupid, right?"

Caldwell said nothing.

"Don't worry, I haven't told anyone, except Orsen, but that's mostly to keep him in line."

"Yes I'm quite familiar with Mr. Orsen's proclivity for the adolescent." He made it sound like a casual tendency rather than a felony.

"Well it makes sense at any rate, them choosing you. You seem trustworthy and objective, unlike the rest of us."

"Mr. Vault, I understand that you're the only one of us who was not given a choice to join this group."

"That's a fair way to put it," Vault replied. "I mean, I was *asked*, and I technically could have said no. But being given the opportunity to decline something is only the illusion of choice. In reality, Abra made sure that I would say yes."

"She threatened you?"

Vault averted his eyes. "Not directly, but the implication was clear."

Ana Leigh opened Caldwell's office door and stepped in.

"Oh, I'm sorry," she said, seeing Vault. "I didn't mean to interrupt, but this came for you."

She handed Caldwell the envelope that the skinny man had given to her. Caldwell stepped over to his desk and took a letter opener to the envelope.

"What is it?" Ana asked.

"It's an invitation," Vault answered. "Isn't it?"

Caldwell looked up. Vault was correct. In addition to the formal invitation, the envelope contained train tickets and what looked like a hotel key-card.

"It's from Smith." Caldwell's voice was hollow. "Ana, would you mind giving Mr. Vault and I some privacy?"

"Of course," she said, shooting Caldwell a concerned look before stepping out and pulling the door closed behind her.

Caldwell set the invitation down.

"How did you know?"

"Because none of this makes sense," Vault explained. "Why would *we* be put in charge? Do you honestly believe that people like Orsen and Coin should be in charge of a world-wide shadow government? No. We were all recruited. I was recruited by Dr. Abra, and you were recruited by Liam Nguyen. *Those* are the people on the inner circle. We're just a front, baubles in a curio case to keep the companies united. Think about it—Mr. Alice has never shown up to one of these board meetings. The Glover Group's Board of Directors is just a deep secret that keeps the real board, the deeper secret, one layer further in the shadows."

Caldwell sighed at sat behind his desk. "Yes, I had suspected that such a group might exist, though I didn't realize how formalized it would be."

"Let me guess, they've invited you to the real Board now that you're co-chairing the fake one."

"It would appear so," replied Caldwell.

Vault stood and walked over to Caldwell's desk, placing both hands down on the desktop. "This is great. It's a chance to shake the whole thing up. They put you on the Board to keep our accounts in check, but what they won't realize is that you'll be there to influence them on our behalf!"

"And why," Caldwell uttered slowly, "would I do that?"

"Listen to me, we can change everything. There are things I know about Mr. Alice. Awful things."

"We *all* know awful things—and they mean nothing. Mr. Vault, we're not men playing with other men. We're dealing with gods now, and their rules are of another order of magnitude. They don't trouble themselves with the petty moralities of mortals. The best we can hope for is to remain on their good side, to enjoy the benefits of the bastards. We're demigods now, you and I, Mr. Vault."

"Aren't all demigods bastards too?" Vault asked, straightening himself.

"Yes," Caldwell said, "and the important thing is that everyone already knows that. This is the new order for us but not for the rest of the world." He stood from behind his desk and lifted his briefcase. "One day Mr. Alice will die, and there will be someone there to take his place. The machine keeps moving."

"So what, you're just going to show up to the meeting and do what they tell you?"

Caldwell tipped his hat. "That's my job, Mr. Vault."

When Caldwell walked out, Vault looked down at the desk and noticed a file. He grabbed it and ran out of the office.

"Caldwell!" he called out. The man was already down the hall awaiting the elevator. "You left this behind!"

"Keep it," said Caldwell, as Vault approached. "It's my file on you. It's empty. You're the only one I don't need to keep tabs on. I don't have to worry that you will be a liability. Keep it that way, Mr. Vault."

Vault watched as Caldwell entered the elevator. He opened the file and could tell at a glance that every secret of his life was somewhere in those pages. Had it been a few months earlier, Vault might've questioned how anyone had acquired such detailed information about him. But he had seen behind the curtain now, and it was hardly surprising.

"Mr. Vault."

He looked up at Caldwell.

"Do you trust me?"

Vault nodded, and the man locked eyes with him. They said more to one another in that moment, as the elevator door shut between them, than they had in all their meetings and dealings combined.

Vault noticed a black-suited man walking past him, the sort that followed he and Orsen around wherever they went. When the man was out of sight and around the corner, Vault looked in the file a second time. There were pictures of his former associates, partners, lovers, and employers, copies of receipts and ledgers and reports from his clinics. There were records of prescription drugs that he himself had forgotten about. Then, among all his life, there was a picture of Caldwell and a profile on the accountant. Caldwell's height and weight were listed, and some previous addresses, nothing substantial. The number that stood out to Vault was the man's age. Could it be true?

Then Caldwell's words echoed in Vault's ears, *one day, Mr. Alice will die, and there will be someone there to take his place, and suddenly,* for the first time since his meeting with Dr. Abra, he felt a sense of relief.

They have scales and they bite, their teeth are sharp, and they stare at you and don't care that they do it, and they wriggle and they writhe and their mouth is agape and their spine is soft and they slither in their slickness under ice and in rivers and they wriggle and they writhe and they dive.

Men are trout.

Acknowledgements

...to my cohort, to David Connor, Giovan Alonzi, Amanda Choo Quan, M Kennedy Volcofsy, Sophie Reiff, Robert Merritt, Vanessa Baish, Julia Lans Nowak, to Leann Rachel Lo and to **emi**, and to all of you in all of the workshops. Thank you Nessa Cannon for sitting through my reading you all these stories, and for listening. My profound thanks to Brian Evenson and Janet Sarbanes for guiding me, to Maggie Nelson and Janice Lee for your wisdom, and all the staff, students, and faculty at CalArts for everything weird and inspiring and critical.

JG VanDenKooy is a writer, composer, and designer.

A graduate of The Herb Alpert School of Music, he holds a BFA in Composition and Digital Arts, and an MFA in Creative Writing from the School of Critical Studies at the California Institute of the Arts (CalArts).

Other Works
By JG VanDenKooy

Fae Daemonologie: The Book of Faolan

Daemonologie: The Book of Keane

The World is Among Us

The Midnight Orchestra

The radio production of The Castle in the Sea

can be found online at jkoi.art

along with other things too.

www.ingramcontent.com/pod-product-compliance
Lightning Source LLC
Chambersburg PA
CBHW060216180626
46813CB00007B/2851